THE UNINVITED TRAVELER: IN THE SHADOW OF TRUMP

By

Ron Breazeale Ph.D

COPYRIGHT PAGE FOR Ron Breazeale, PhD. (The Uninvited Traveler: In the Shadow of Trump)

Copyright page

Publisher's Name: Ron Breazeale, PhD.

ISBN: 978-1-962142-30-4

Contents

CHAPTER 1

I'd been thinking about it for months, maybe years. Planning, you could say. I played it through in my mind dozens of times.

Rehearsed what I was going to say over and over. Practiced on the long drives to and from the office. But the only living creature who'd heard the full monologue was Walter. He always seemed interested when I talked to him. I'm sure that's because I talked to him like he was a human being. And, you know, I guess I feel like he is, sort of, even though he's a Golden Retriever.

As for real human beings, I talked to Joe, my best friend, about what I was planning. Well, not seriously. I talked to him seriously about how tired I was of my life. How it had to change. Tired, bored, stressed out: I couldn't find the right words. Like Walter, he seemed to understand. But, unlike Walter, I never really told him about my plan. I'm sure Joe would have said, "Go for it." I'm positive that he was tired of hearing me complain. But he's different from me, more willing to take risks. Joe often refers to me as "a man of caution." I think he means it as a compliment. At least I hope so.

On good days, I told myself that I was just being careful. I didn't want to lose everything I'd worked on for so long. And how would I feel if I left her? Bad is what came to mind every time I tried. Scared. The fear always took over.

I remember many times when things would happen to start me up again. She'd say or do something, and I'd start thinking about how I couldn't take it anymore and had to leave. I usually wouldn't sayanything. She'd ask, "Are you upset, Lou? Are you mad about something I said?"

But I'd deny it. "No, I just didn't have a very good day at work."

She'd give up and we'd continue on. Usually, that's as far asit went. It was just in my head. I seldom said or did anything aboutit. Oh, I'd talk with Walter about it, or maybe my friend Joe. But it was just thinking and maybe some talking. No real action. A couple of times, I got to the point of packing. But my hands would start sweating, my heart would beat really fast, and I'd begin to feel dizzy, so I'd unpack.

I mean, I had a lot of reasons to stay. We have a nice house. Even though the girls are out on their own, they still come to visit.

And Lynn, I know she loves me. You may find it hard to believe, because of what I finally decided to do, but I love her, too.

Could I have faced Lynn? Told her I was leaving? I don't think so. Itried to talk about it a few times. I remember saying, "I don't think we're very happy together anymore." She'd say, "Well, you know, we could go to marriage counseling. I think that would help," and I wouldn't respond. I guess I never wanted to go when it might've helped. I didn't think it would work. And it didn't when she finally convinced me to go for a few sessions. The woman counselorseemed to me to take Lynn's side from the start. Maybe she hadn't. But I started making up excuses for not going, and Lynn finally gaveup.

On bad days, I'd call myself a coward. And all sorts of other names. I'd say that I didn't have the guts to leave. On those days, I'd tell myself that I should find a good reason. Our girls are grown and living their lives out in the Midwest. And Lynn has friends. Manymore than I do. She also has a career that she'd never leave—notfor me or anyone else. And who am I to ask her to? She pushes herself hard. Says that she doesn't know how much time she has. Her diabetes is getting worse, already robbing her of the feeling in the tips of her fingers and toes. She's sure that it'll eventually come for her eyesight. Every day counts.

So I asked myself, "Does every day count for me?" I wasn't sure.I just knew that I couldn't keep doing what I was doing every day. I've been an accountant for most of my life—well, really just a bookkeeper; I didn't take the test to become an accountant. I like numbers. They're precise. Clear. Clean. There are answers to problems. Precise ones. I've always liked that. And that was enough for me, even when there were no answers to things happening outside my work cubicle. I tried to figure them out, but I didn't seem to have the patience or whatever it takes. I just usually retreated into my safe place, my numbers. Until the last few months.

I saw her again a couple of months ago. That's when my planning really started. We hadn't talked in many years, and it was just bychance that we met. I stopped at the 7-Eleven on my way home.

I needed milk. I think it was milk. Yes, I'm sure it was milk. Anyway, she was there, standing in the checkout line. I think she had a quart of orange juice. I'm not sure. She saw me and spokefirst. If she hadn't, I don't know what I would've done. She asked, "How are you?" as if she really meant it. I lied. "Fine." I smiled. I didn't know what to say, so I said something dumb like, "It's been a long time." No kidding, twenty years. She stepped out of line and came over to where I was standing. She said that she was glad to finally be back home. She was working in a friend's toy shop downtown. She said that she really didn't have time to talk then but would love to catch up. She asked me to call her and gave me her phone number. She bought the orange juice and was gone.

Over the last twenty years, I'd thought of her often. Thoughtabout calling her, looking her up on the Internet. But, you know, I never did. I was afraid. I didn't know what to say. Most of all, I didn't know what she would say. I didn't want to take the chance of her rejecting me, not responding to my email, or telling me not to call her again. Nothing was better than that.

I drove the rest of the way home that night in a bit of a daze. When I got there, my wife said, "You look horrible." I just grunted a response. Lynn and I didn't talk very much that night. We never do anymore. Like most other nights, she watched her shows: CSI, ER, etc. I pretended to read. But I wasn't reading. My mind was on whathad happened.

Lynn tried to make conversation. "What are you reading now, Lou?" I didn't respond at first. I wasn't paying attention. "Lou!"

"Oh, just another Civil War book." I loved reading about the Civil War. It took me away from the one that she and I had been fightingfor so many years.

"Oh." She wasn't a fan of Civil War books.

I went to bed before her, as usual, and kissed her forehead. She seemed to barely notice.

I couldn't sleep. Like I said, that was the night I really started planning this whole thing. Well, not the whole thing; a lot happened that I hadn't planned. Boy, a whole lot!

So, you're probably wondering what I was planning. In fact, you'veprobably already guessed. But let me tell you that—and why— and then I'll tell you what happened. About Thomas and the others.They weren't part of the plan.

Oh, I forgot to introduce myself: Louis Black here. I'm sixty-two and three months. Married—obviously. Two daughters, ages twenty-eight and twenty-six. They're married but have no children yet. I'd certainly like to have some grandchildren, but I'm not sure that my wife is ready. One of our many disagreements. We've been marrieda long time. Too long. Happily? Not for many years. Have I known what to do about that? Not a clue.

Now, don't get me wrong. Lynn is a good woman. She was a good mother and has a right to her career. But with the kids gone, it seems like her career takes all her time; she doesn't have much gasleft in her tank at the end of the day. For me or for anyone else. Iguess you could blame that on the diabetes. That's what I toldmyself. But maybe she just wasn't interested in me. Maybe beingwith me or talking with me just didn't appeal to her anymore. Atleast she gave me that feeling. When I'd try to touch her, she'dpull away. She certainly seemed to have no interest in sex with me.Or anyone else, I assumed.

So, I was planning on leaving it all. We had the money. I'd leave the house to Lynn and the kids. Lynn had come into some money when her parents had died. With what I could provide, she'd be okay. After all these years, the mortgage was almost paid off— exactly

$10,336 left. I didn't think I'd need much money to be happy. To be exact, $26,385 a year.

I just wanted something different. I was sick of it all. The job. AndI found less and less of life interesting each day. Or the marriage, for that matter. I was tired of trying to work things out. Tired of nothingchanging. Lynn loved the self-help books. She was always giving meone to read. Sometimes, I'd page through it. I didn't really have the time, I thought, to read it. And she'd ask me about it. She always wanted to do the exercises they recommended.

"Lou, have you made your list?""What list?"

"The things you're grateful for, Lou.""Oh yeah," I'd say, "I forgot."

"I thought you were the one who wanted to make things better in this marriage."

"Well, I do. I just forgot. Don't make a federal case out of it." But Iforgot a lot. So, I stumbled along. But I was getting more tired every day. Of everything. Something **had** to change.

So, I began to plan. I wanted to go someplace warm. I hate New England winters. Start over. Some people do, you know. Some of my friends have. I could draw out some of my retirement and actually do it. The kids would understand. Even Lynn would understand. ButI really didn't want to do it by myself. I didn't want to start over with that again. I felt too old. What would be the point of dating? Just to not be alone?

That's when Jay reappeared in my life for the third time that night at the 7-Eleven. Like I said, I'd thought about her over the years. The choices we'd made. We'd been young. Really young. In our twenties—well, late twenties. You know, I never knew how much she cared for me until it ended. It was a little late to find out. I'd made other plans; they were all in place.

Years passed. I married Lynn. We had our first child, then our second.

I've often debated with myself about whether I should've left the relationship with Jay. Let it end the first time. The answer wasalways yes. At the time, it seemed that we wanted different things: Iwanted a family; she wanted a career. It was the reverse with Lynn. She wanted a family. Her career at that time wasn't as important. Funny how things have changed.

We kept talking after we broke up, and even met for lunch when we could. One day at lunch, she told me. She said things she'd never said when we were together. Like that, she'd thought we'd always be together. Just straight out of the blue, there it was. I didn't know what to say or do. So, true to my nature, I said and did nothing. I don't know what she thought. We didn't talk for a while. I finally called her, and we had lunch again. We just went on. But something had changed. She had excuses f o r why she couldn't meet again. And then she moved to California, and we lost contact. She did return to Maine for a few years, three, and we saw each other again. We actually worked together for a year. And more than that. But she justup and quit and moved back to L.A. Joe said that maybe shejust couldn't take working so close to me every day, having the affair,but me staying with Lynn. I don't know. She didn't tell me whatwas going on. She barely even said goodbye when she left.

I continued to think about her. On my way to the office, I used to pass an old stone church that was used mainly for weddings and funerals. I'd imagine her in a white wedding gown, coming down the steps with me. She was beautiful. It was beautiful. But I couldn'tthink about that very much, just for a few seconds. I felt . . . well, Idon't know what I felt.

So that was it. No letters, no phone calls, nothing for years.

It took me a few days, but I called. Asked her to lunch, like old times. But things were different from the last time. I was looking for something, something I hadn't seen or felt in years. And I started to find it. Oh, I continued to lie, but she knew that I was lying. We began to make up reasons to meet. We talked. We always could talk, although she talked a lot more than I did.

"You know, I got married a few years after we stopped seeingeach other. I put my career on hold for a while. He supported bothof us, but I wasn't happy. I needed to work, so I took a job in retail as a manager. The hours were long, too long for him, which I can understand. I was always gone evenings and weekends. He finally had enough of it, so we split. Eventually, I got sick of it myself, so I quit and came back home. I didn't have any ties there. We neverhad children."

She sounded like she regretted that. She didn't have much family left. Just a sister that she seldom talked to or saw.

"So, I reconnected with my friend Barbara. I live with her, which has been good so far."

But she sounded like she wanted something else. Like me, she seemed sick of it all. That's why she'd come back.

Our lunches began to give me some hope, and I hadn't felt hope ina long time. But things stayed in the same place. We didn't take it to another level. We were just old friends getting together for lunch at least until one Thursday when she started talking about Florida

"It was down in the 30s last night, Lou."

"Yeah, I know," I said. "The almanac says it's going to be a cold, snowy winter."

"God, I hope not. I hate the cold. People in the store yesterday were talking about getting ready to go to Florida after the holidays. Iwish I could."

"I'm with you, Jay. I'm not sure I can take another winter like the last one. I'm not sure I can take many more."

"I don't think that rentals in Florida are as expensive as they used to be. You know, the cost of living is a lot cheaper down there."

We kept talking. We talked about how much fun it would be to walk on the beach in the morning. We both like seafood. Redsnapper.

We enjoyed the conversation and the fantasy of running away toFlorida. But I guess I took it more seriously than she did. I showed up at our next lunch with a bunch of travel brochures. Hey, I started to take action. Me, taking action, believe it or not.

I began rehearsing the plan I'd had in my head for a long time. Myconversation with my boss, the call I'd make to my daughters, the letter I'd leave for Lynn. I checked my accounts. Went over the numbers. The financial plan was good. But, most importantly, the conversation I would have with Jay—that was the hardest part of theplan. I needed to talk with her first.

CHAPTER 2

I decided that I'd wait for her to finish work and ask her to have a drink or coffee. I just couldn't wait until the next lunch. If I didn't do it soon, I was afraid that I wouldn't do it at all.

I couldn't sleep that night. Finally, just before sunrise, I took Walter out for a walk. I told him what I was going to do. That I'd be leaving and wouldn't see him again. He was really Lynn and the kids' dog, as well as mine, and I would've felt guilty if I'd taken him. God knows I felt guilty about enough. I told him that I'd miss him and our conversations. And I certainly would. But I thought it was best if I tried to put him out of my mind, along with a lot of other things. God that was hard, saying goodbye to that damn dog. One of the hardest things I've ever done.

As we were coming back, I saw a blue-white flash in the sky. It silently trailed off to the east. A meteor, I thought. I wasn't really into paying much attention to the sky, but the flash was awfully bright and seemed close.

Lynn was still asleep. She always looked so peaceful when she slept. I left the letter for her on my bureau. I assumed that she wouldn't find it for a while. She never bothered my personal stuff. But I knew that she'd get curious after a while and start looking. I'd call in the next day or two and tell her where the letter was and what I was doing. I'd call when it was unlikely that she'd pick up.

I drove to work, listening to the radio, like I always did. A lot of people had reported a bright light in the sky that morning. The weather service said that it was probably just a meteor. Maybe part of it had actually struck Earth near where we were living; some people had reported the sound of a crash. But I wasn't interested in all that. I had some work to do to get ready to leave.

Don't get me wrong, I've always kept organized at work. But I wanted to leave things in a really good way. The firm deserved that from me, after all these years. I didn't talk to him, but I left a letter for my boss, explaining what I was doing and why. I said he could call me if he had any questions.

You know, in all those years, I never made many friends at work. Always had my lunch in my cubicle. I doubted that anyone would really miss me. Maybe my boss. He knew I was a good worker. Maybe Jim. We used to talk politics. He was a big Trumper.

I finished up work early, seeing my last client at 2:00. He'd driven in from Winterpool. Dr. Lee Brazil, a psychologist. I'd been working with him over the last year to straighten out his taxes. He'd failed to file on time a number of years ago and had backtaxes and penalties. But he had a good excuse. He'd been involvedin an accident at a nuclear facility, Pine Grove, in eastern Tennessee. Initially, he and another friend from Maine were accused of being part of a terrorist plot. It was in all the papers. They'd held the poor bastard in detention while they sorted the whole thing out. Meanwhile, real terrorists had taken advantage of the accident to create a real disaster. Parts of the area are still abandoned. And much of what happened there is still classified,top secret. They released him a couple of years ago, but they've been hounding him about his taxes ever since. It's a little hard tofile your taxes if you're in the slammer.

I know what I'm telling you because I read the papers. He's always been pretty tight-lipped about what happened. We usuallyjust focused on the numbers, which was fine with me. I think he should be okay now. I tried my best to tie up loose ends with him and the office. And I left.

I waited in my car in the parking lot outside the store where she worked. It was late November, and dark already at four o'clock. I hate the dark. And it was cold, too. I felt like—well, I guess I felt likea damn stalker, although I'm not really sure how stalkers feel.

I was packed. The car was packed. I'd been very careful. Taken only what I'd thought I might need. It had been easy in some ways. I'd packed the car after Lynn had gone to bed.

I kept going through what I was going to say, so much so that I missed Jay leaving the store. It was dark, and my eyes kept watering.

She was pulling out of the parking lot. I could've blown the horn or waved, but, for some reason, I didn't. I just followed her. She didn't see me. She drove down Main Street and stopped at the same 7/Eleven where we'd met a few months before.

She pulled in and parked. I pulled in and parked. She saw me and smiled. She looked surprised and came over to the car. I rolled the window down and blurted out something like, "I need to talk to you" or "We need to talk." Whatever I said made her look worried. I said I was sorry and to get in the car. She did and noticed the stuff in the backseat—my bags, and a cooler. She asked what I was doing. I tried to answer. I launched into, "I just can't do it anymore." "Oh, Lou," she said. "What are you going to do?"

"I don't know. Leave it all behind."

She looked puzzled as to what to say next. "Are you sure?" "As sure as I'll ever be."

"Where are you going?" "Florida," I said.

I noticed him out of the corner of my eye. He was looking at us. I ignored him and looked down at my hands. They were shaking.

"Oh, Lou," she said again. "Are you sure this is what you want?"

Just as I was about to ask, "Will you go with me?" the back door of my car opened. I thought I'd locked it. I was sure I'd locked it. The strange-looking fellow who'd been standing by the door to the 7/Eleven was pushing his way into my backseat. I turned around, but, before I could say anything, he ordered, "I need to go to Florida. Drive." And he pointed this black thing at me. I don't remember what happened next. I think I said something like—well, I don't remember. And Jay didn't say anything, either.

The next thing I remember was being on the highway, Interstate 95, heading south. I must've driven an hour before knowing what I was doing. I'm still not sure. Maybe I blacked out mentally. I guess that's what you'd call it. But it was more than that. His voice was in my head.

At first, I was really scared. I mean my hands were shaking and my heart was beating really hard. But the thing that freaked me out most was that voice. His voice.

Who was this nut job in my backseat? Did he have a gun or something? Well, he had something. I wasn't sure what it was, but he had it and had pointed it at me.

No one was saying anything. I kept trying to get a look at this guy, but the rearview mirror couldn't pick him up. He was leaning against the door with his head down.

I felt like stopping and confronting him, telling him to get out ofmy frigging car. But that voice in my head said, "Don't." It wasn'tmy voice. It was his.

I wasn't in control of what was happening, and not being incontrol had always scared me. I think I've been scared most of my life. Ever since I was a little kid. I don't really know why. I guess if I really think about it, it goes back to those screaming matches that my parents used to have. If I close my eyes, I can see myself on theold brown couch in our living room underneath the pillows. I can stillhear them. "What the hell have you been doing all day? You been hanging around with that bunch of women who always badmouth me? Don't you walk away from me! I'm talking to you!"

"What's it to you? I fixed supper for you tonight, and where were you? Hanging out in Ron's pub with your drinking buddies."

"There you go again. I can't have a drink after work and unwind a little bit?"

"You know it's not just one drink. It's five or six! We don't have themoney for you to go out on the town every night!"

"Well, if you'd get a job and stop hanging out with your girlfriends we could afford to move out of this dump!"

It would go on like that. She'd throw a plate of food at him, and he'd slap her. He scared the hell out of me. I thought he might kill her. That's when I'd try to tune out. I couldn't do anything about it. Ihad no control. Some nights the neighbors would call the police, but they'd just calm things down and leave. Nothing ever changed, until he finally left.

That was a lot of years ago. But it seems like just yesterday. Idon't like talking about it. I don't even like thinking about it. I justget worked up. But I began to notice that this time, I didn't feel as upset as usual. Not about things in the past, or what was happening in the present. I wasn't feeling scared anymore. Strangely, a part of me felt relieved. I didn't have to take the risk of asking Jay to gowith me. We were driving to Florida, just as I'd hoped. Well, not exactly. Where in Florida we were going, I wasn't sure, but that didn't seem to matter at the moment.

He'd been very precise in giving me direction: "Turn here. Speed up.Slow down," he said aloud. That's all he said at first. His directions feltlike commands. They got inside my head, and it was like I couldn't doanything else but what he wanted. What he'd said kept echoing in my head: "Drive." "Drive." "Drive."

I tried to say something, but he ordered silence, and we complied.I looked at Jay. She gave me one of her "I don't know what to do,do you?" looks. I responded in kind.

We drove on, slipped through the Maine tolls, and crossed the bridge into Portsmouth. A few minutes later, we were coming off the bridge, and I saw the exit to downtown. Exit 1. I thought about taking it but couldn't decide. We passed it. We passed the second and third exits. I felt like I couldn't make a decision if my life depended on it. As the lights of Portsmouth faded into the distance, I thought about Lynn. Maybe she would've found my letter by now.

She'd be upset but would assume that I was doing what I felt was necessary. At least I hoped she'd feel that way. She'd wait before doing anything. She wouldn't report me missing, because I'd told her what I was doing and where I was going. She might expect me to change my mind and call her in a day or two. I'd left before and had come back with my tail between my legs.

I started thinking about the last time I'd spoken to Lynn. It seemed impossible that it was just this morning. I'd called her at work. I'd thought for a second that I might tell her about my plan.

She answered her extension after a number of rings, and the conversation if, if you could call it that, went as it often did.

"How are you, honey?" I asked."I'm fine. What do you need?"

I almost said, "A hell of a lot more than we have right now," but I didn't. Instead, I said my usual: "Nothing. I just wanted to hear your voice and know that you're okay."

"I'm okay, Lou." She sounded irritated. "But I'm real busy. I got a call holding on the other line. I'll be home late tonight."

"I know," I said. "You and the girls are going out." "We are not girls, Lou, we're women."

"Yeah, yeah," I said, adding, "whatever," under my breath."I'll see you when I get home," she said.

"Okay, goodbye honey."

Lynn and I were never very good on the phone. I always felt rushed.

One of the things I loved about Jay was that we could havenormal conversations. She usually had time to talk for a minute or two and always had something to tell me. I liked that.

Unfortunately, I'd done a lot of comparing the two over the past few months, which hasn't been good for my relationship with Lynn.

As for Jay, I wasn't sure. She really had no family, no one who'dbe checking on her. She had some friends, but she was a very private person. Bottom line, we wouldn't be missed. At least not fora while. So, it was just the two of us . . . and the guy in the backseat.

When we entered Massachusetts, he told me to turn onto Route 495, and I did. I'd filled the car with gas before I'd met up with Jay, so we could go about five or six hours without stopping. For gas, at least. Of course, there were other reasons for stopping. Like for a restroom or food. I made some weak efforts at conversation with our passenger. "Hey, I don't know who you are, but if you'll let us go at the next rest stop, you can have the car. We won't press charges."

Jay turned around and gave him one of her most sincere looks. "Honest. Lou's right. We won't press charges. We won't even call the cops."

But his only answer was "Drive."

By midnight, I'd had it. The adrenaline or whatever was wearing off. I told him we had to stop at the next rest area. Jay was wiggling around in her seat and giving me desperate looks. We both neededa bathroom badly. He said nothing, so I took matters into my own hands and turned onto the next rest-stop exit. That was a big step for me. I thought he'd yell or hit me or do something, but he just waited.

I guess that I'd calmed down some. I'd been counting road signs. Yes, road signs. I told you, I like numbers. When I'm upset, I count things. It's always worked for me. There are thirty-nine road signs on the Massachusetts Turnpike between the Worcester and New York exits.

And I'll tell you something about Jay that she'd never admit. She always wears her mother's engagement ring, and I can tell when she's nervous or upset because she starts twisting it. I've never toldher that I noticed. She'd only deny it. We've all got those things we do to calm down. I count things. Jay twists her mother's ring.

I pulled into the rest area and turned around to our passenger. "We both need some sleep, but I need a bathroom first." Jay noddedin agreement.

"You go," he ordered, pointing at me. "You wait," he said to Jay.

I guess he figured I'd come back. What else could I do? Unfortunately, and to my surprise, no one else was around. He took our cell phones before he let me leave the car. I went in and looked for an attendant. I'd chosen an exit that had a travel information center, so I thought there might be one. But no attendant. I looked for a payphone. The only one I found was next to the women's bathroom and looked like it hadn't worked in years. Someone had torn the guts out of the receiver.

When Jay left the car, I again turned around to get a better look at our passenger, but I couldn't. His head was down and he pulled the hoody up tight around his face. He was leaning against the door. I began to think that he was hurt, so I asked, "Are you okay?"

He didn't answer. I asked again. No answer. "If you need a doctor, we'll take you to one."He just looked down. No response.

Jay wasn't gone long. She joined me in staring blankly and waitingfor his next command.

"Sleep," he said. So, we tried.

I took the initiative again and pulled Jay as close to me as Icould with the bucket seats. It had been years since I'd felt herbody next to mine. She was warm and soft, just like so manyyears before. I tried not to think. I let out a huge sigh and fell intoa deep sleep. I was always good at sleeping. Lynn said it was my escape. She said I could sleep through a hurricane. I think I actually did once. But I didn't sleep very long, even though I wasdog tired.

As it was starting to get light, our friend in the backseat touched my arm. His hand was cold, very cold, but his touch was gentle, almost apologetic. I opened my eyes and turned to look at him. His hoody was still pulled down over his head, but I caught a glimpse of him. His complexion looked almost gray. No beard, or hair that I could see. The expression on his face—well, I don't know how to describe it. His eyes were larger than any I'd ever seen on a human being. I didn't say anything. I just turned back around and waited. "Drive," he said.

"Okay, okay, but I need the bathroom first." He motioned for me to go, so I slipped out.

Still no one around. I tried to find another phone or someone again. I located another pay phone, but it was like the first one. I was afraid to stay too long because of Jay. I was feeling desperate again, but I guess that was good because I decided right then and there that I was going to do something to force him to talk, whetherhe wanted to or not.

When I got back to the car, it was Jay's turn to go to the bathroom and my turn to start a round of twenty questions.

"How long have you been in this country?" I asked, figuring that since he was a man of few words he might be still learning our language. I stared at him.

"Not long," he said, almost in a whisper.

Now we're getting somewhere, I thought. "So where are youfrom?" I asked.

He hesitated then replied, "A long distance from here." He slidback into the seat suddenly, like he was in pain.

I asked him again, "Are you okay?"

"No," he said, again in a low whisper. "I think you need to see a doctor."

"No," he responded. "A doctor cannot help me."

Jay was back. She opened the passenger door and slipped backinside. I looked at her.

"He's hurt," I said. "He needs to see a doctor.""No," he said again. "Drive."

So, I started the car. We drove back onto the interstate andcontinued south.

CHAPTER 3

I waited an hour before speaking again. It was mid-morning, and I was hungry. We were in upstate New York, near the town of Fishkill. I used to stop there when I drove south to visit friends, so I knew where I could find a gas station and diner.

"Look, mister. We haven't eaten since noon yesterday. Can we stopand get some food? You must be hungry, too."

"No, I am not hungry, but, yes, you may stop," he said.

I drove off the exit and was trying to figure out what to do when he touched my arm. "Here," he said, handing me what looked like two small blue crystals.

"You may go in and get your food, but you must carry these with you at all times."

"You stay with me," he said, pointing the black box at Jay.

"Okay," I said. I didn't know what to make of this homeless guy. He must be psychotic. Delusional. Blue crystals and that black . . . box.

"Say nothing about me."

"Okay," I repeated. His words echoed in my brain like commands. He was in my head again, and . . . I still didn't know . . . well, what to do. I felt like just going along with his wishes.

I went into the diner. It wasn't very crowded. A waitress came over.

"Do you want to see a menu?"

I didn't say anything at first. I was still thinking about what to do.

His voice was distracting me."Sir?"

"Yes. Take out, I think." I looked at the waitress, a young womanwith a bad case of acne. She smiled.

"What can I get you?"

I didn't say anything. She waited.

"A couple of hamburgers, I guess. Fries. And two coffees withcream."

"With everything?"

I nodded. In what seemed like only a minute, she was back withthe food. When I came out of the diner, Jay was sitting at a picnic table nearthe car.

I put the food down on the table and didn't say anything. Before I could, Jay blurted out, "I just couldn't take sitting in the car any longer. With him. He said it was okay for us to sit out here and eat."

I opened the bag and started putting the food out. "I got you a hamburger and some fries and coffee."

"He's looking at us," she said.

I wasn't sure why, but I wanted to defend him. "He hasn't done anything except hitch a ride with us. He hasn't threatened us. He hasn't hurt us."

"Well, he scares the bejesus out of me. I just can't think clearly… with that… with him and that black thing. What the hell is that? He keeps pointing it at us like it has…some kind of magic."

"Maybe it does," I said. "I don't know. Maybe he's just crazy. Maybe I'm crazy, but I feel like he's harmless. I'm not afraid of him." But that wasn't completely true. "He's harmless," I repeated, hoping that he was. "If he were going to do anything to us, he would've already." "Since when are you the expert on homeless people who hitch rides to Florida?"

"Well, we know he won't get there if we turn him over to the police. I just have a feeling that we shouldn't turn him in. Besides, I think he's hurt."

"You and your feelings," Jay responded, sounding disgusted. "So, I'm supposed to spend my week off as a nursemaid to a crazy man?" She shook her head. "I don't think so."

"You have the week off? I didn't know that. That's great!""Hey, there are a lot of things you don't know about me."

She was right. She wasn't a talkative person when she was the subject. She could rattle on about all sorts of things, but when the conversation got serious and turned to her, she was great at changing the subject. I remembered one of the last times we talked, really talked, at the Greek place. We were having lunch,and I asked her, "Do you have a bucket list, honey?"

"What do you mean?"

"I mean things you want to do before you die."She paused. "I don't know. Do you?"

"I've told you about some of the things I want to do. But I'm asking about you." "You want to travel, Lou. Right? To Europe. You've never beenthere."

"I told you before that I'd love to see Paris with you. And don't tellme I can't afford it I've saved some money."

She rolled her eyes and didn't say anything, just like she did whenI said this the first time.

"But what do you want to do, Jay?"

"Well, Europe would be nice I guess but expensive. You know, I'mokay with what I have here. The way things are these days in the world, I'm not sure I want to leave the good old USA."

And so it went. I didn't ask again. I guess I felt hurt. Like shedidn't trust me. And maybe she didn't. I'd let her down big time in the past. Maybe she didn't feel that she could trust me anymore with her dreams.

There might be a lot that I still didn't know about Jay, but I did know one thing: "I don't want to go back," I said, looking down at the table. "And I don't want you to go back. I want you to go . . . to go with me."

"I don't know, Lou. This is all so crazy.""All?" I asked. "No, not that part," she replied. "This." She gestured toward the car. "Just figure out a way to call the police. They can take him to a hospital, then you and I can decide what we want to do."

I finished my food or at least most of it. I didn't have much of an appetite. I began to feel that I should go back to the car right then.

"Just let me talk to him before we call the police or do anything else. Maybe he's got family we can call," I said.

Jay shook her head again and muttered, "Crazy, crazy, crazy. God, I just can't think straight this morning. It's that black box, isn't it?He's using it on us, isn't he? What is he, CIA?"

"I don't know, Jay. I don't know. Maybe. But I can't think of anything else to do right now but what he says. If we don't, I don't know what will happen." And I didn't. "Just eat your hamburger. I'll talk to him."

"I'm not getting in that car again. I'm not going another mile with this guy until you show me why should."

"Fair enough," I said. "Give me fifteen minutes."

As soon as I opened the driver's door, our passenger began totalk.

"I have much to explain to you. Time is short. I am here on a mission. My people have just communicated with me." "Great." Now he's hearing voices.

"They will be here sooner than I expected. They will need myhelp, but I am not well."

I could certainly agree with that.

"We have no time to deal with your police."Had he been reading our lips? I wondered."I am, indeed, a homeless person."

"Now we're getting somewhere," I said.

"But not as you believe. My people and I are homeless. We have been expelled from our homeland and are seeking a new one."

"So, you're immigrants, asylum seekers. I imagine that's very difficult for anyone. I know how it feels when people treat you like you don't belong. Like they're better than you." I was thinking about how a number of people at my old job had treated me. The accountants with their certifications and me just a lowly bookkeeper.

"Yes," he said. "The new life forms that we created no longer haveneed of us."

Oh, God, here we go into crazy talk. I decided to play along."What new life forms?"

"The machines that you call computers. The old ones say thattheir . . . I think you would call it 'take over' of our world began when we stopped teaching our children to do for themselves basic mathematics. It progressed rapidly from there. The machines were better problem solvers than we were. They could think more clearly;their logic was not clouded by emotion. At first, life was much betterfor us. But we were no longer producing anything of value, and it was not long until the machines decided that we no longer served any useful purpose. They determined that we were a drain on our planet's energy sources, which are very limited."

"Now, wait a minute," I said. "You lost me after the homeless part. If we're going to get anywhere, you need to stop talking crazy."

"I assure you; I am not talking . . . crazy. What must I do to prove this to you?"

"I don't know." I shrugged.

"Here," he pushed his black box into my hands. "Look at the screen."

I did and, to my amazement, saw Jay still sitting at the picnic table where I'd left her. He touched the box, and I could see inside the restaurant.

"Do you see your police officers in the first booth?" "Yes," I said. I hadn't noticed them when I'd gone in."I will call them away." He touched the box, and the officers' radio buzzed."Okay, so where are you from? Really. The CIA?"

He shook his head.

"Another . . . world," I said, with great hesitation.

"Yes. One that lies on the edge of our shared solar system. Some of your NASA scientists have communicated with our world. That is why you must help me."

I didn't say anything at first. I was, to say the least, surprised, and confused—I didn't have a good word for how I felt. I just looked at him.

Then he said, "As your religious leaders might say, we were created by your God in his image. We are flesh and blood, like you and your people."

"Now, wait a minute. Don't start talking religion to me." My motherhad drilled that stuff into my head. She became a religious nut after my father left. The whole nine yards. Every time the church doorwas open, she was there with me and my brother. I got sick of it. I haven't been in a church since I left home, except to marry Lynn. "I'm not ready for any religious talk." Like I was ready for anything he was saying. "We have studied your planet for many Earth years. We have learned your language and much about your culture—or cultures, I should say. I believe that we can bring much to your world."

"Yeah, that little black box is a nifty thing," I said.

"No," he replied quickly. "We are not allowed to share our technologies. Our masters have forbidden that. We are only allowed to use them to reach your world. Upon our arrival, devices like this will be destroyed. They are programmed to self-destruct shortly after landing."

"Your people created them. Surely your scientists and engineers will know how to make new ones."

"We have no scientists or engineers among our people anymore. The machines made this device. What we can teach your world is the art of coexistence. Tolerance."

I laughed. "That would be a nice trick."He looked confused.

"I mean, that would be good, but I think it would be hard for my people to learn that particular mindset." I was sure that it would be, with or without his magic. Since the last election, no one hadpatience for anyone who didn't agree with them. And if you'd voted for Trump, some people behaved like you had the plague or at least a seriously affected level of intelligence.

Lynn had voted for Clinton. She was all for Hillary and her crew. Bumper stickers and the whole works. She told me not to vote for Trump. She said that I'd regret it, but Jay and I did vote for him. And I haven't really regretted it. Well, not as much as she thought I would.

"Perhaps we have learned these lessons too well," he said, "and that has led to our present dilemma. We have never waged war, butI must warn you, if my people do not find a home on your planet,the machines will not hesitate to destroy us and your world as well."

"Why?" I asked. "They've gotten rid of you and your people. Isn't that what they wanted?"

"Yes, but they do not trust that your people will not attempt to destroy them with your nuclear weapons. Your history is replete with exploration and the conquest and subjugation of humans who are only slightly different from those who lead your race."

He continued to talk about his people and his world, the homethat they had to leave.

Needless to say, I was pretty taken aback. I guess that's what you'd call it. Now, hold on. I know you'll think I'm crazy, but, at that moment, I felt like I was finally being asked to do something that really mattered in the world. You know, something that people would see as important. This poor fellow really needed my help. Maybe he was crazy, with all this talk about "machines," but, then, where did he get that thing he calls a "device," that black box? How could he do all that stuff if he wasn't. . . well, important. I mean, someone to look up to. Listen to. I think I'd never felt important all my life. I'd never really had the opportunity to do something important. Here was my chance, and Jay's, too, and I was going to take it.

I walked back to the picnic table, unsure of what to say. Jay wasall ready to go. On her feet. I sat down, and so did she.

"What took so long? I thought you were only going to be a fewminutes with him. It's been half an hour."

"Everything's fine, honey. It just took longer than I thought itwould."

"What took longer?" she asked.

"We had a lot to talk about. He had a lot to tell me."

"Well, what are we doing? I saw the police leave; we should haveflagged them down."

"Maybe, maybe," I said. "What do you mean, maybe?" "I mean, this guy, he knows a lot of things. More than we think hedoes. He's on a mission."

Jay rolled her eyes.

"It's really important that we try to help him. Trust me on this one." I gave her a look that she says she hates but has a hard time resisting.

"It's not dangerous, is it?" she asked. "He's not strung out ondrugs or something?"

"No. He's got an old friend in Florida he really needs to reconnect with. If we drive straight through, we can be there by tomorrow night. Just come back to the car. I got him talking." How I knew all of this, I wasn't sure. He hadn't told me. I mean, he hadn't said it to me in words. But it was in my head.

I didn't know what else to say. I figured that he might be better at explaining all this.

Before I could get in and close the door, Jay was firing questionsat our homeless alien.

"Who are you?" she asked. "We don't even know your name.""I am a being like yourself. I am flesh and blood like you."

Jay rolled her eyes. "Yes, but what's your name?""You may call me Thomas." "Okay," she said. "And why are you in such a rush to get to Florida?"

"I must see Peter Johnson. It is a matter of extreme importance." "And why must you talk to him?"

"He is employed by the National Aeronautics and Space Administration of your country."

Jay looked confused and a bit disturbed with his answers, so I stepped in.

"He needs to talk about a very important project he's working on. You could say it's a matter of national security." I didn't tell her the truth; I didn't know what she'd do. If I told her all that he'd told me, she'd think that I . . . well . . . that I was crazy, too. Best that it comes straight from him.

Jay gave me one of her "you think I'm buying this?" looks.

She moved toward the door, but I grabbed her arm. "Jay, this is something really big. Please trust me. This is really important."

She hesitated then looked at me. "Okay, Lou. I don't understand what the two of you are up to, but I guess I can go along for the ride for at least the next day and a half. Why I'm agreeing to this I don't know."

I wondered if Thomas was in her head, too. Well, we had at least a name for our passenger. Like Jay, I wasn't completely ready to buy all he'd said. But I was willing to go along for the ride, too. Why? Well, we were going to Florida. Just like I'd wanted.

We pulled back onto the interstate and continued our drive south.

I was still worried about Thomas. I wanted to say something, but I didn't know what. We still hadn't gotten a good look at him because of the hoody, although I'd gotten a glimpse of one hand, and it didn't look good. He also hadn't had anything to eat or drink since we began this trip, so, I decided to try again.

"Thomas, aren't you hungry or thirsty? Doesn't your flesh and blood need some nourishment?"

"No. I have these." He showed us a handful of red and purple pills and pellets.

"Great," said Jay. "I thought you told me he wasn't a druggie.""I am not what you call a 'druggie,'" said Thomas.

"He's not a druggie, Jay," I said with irritation. "But your hand, Thomas, it looks like it's burned." "Yes," he replied. "When our ship overheated on entry to your atmosphere, I sustained a number of burns to my body. The other three members of my crew died from their injuries." He fell silentand pulled down the hoodie further.

Jay looked at me, brows raised. "Oh, for the love of God. A spaceship, Lou?" Really?"

I ignored her. The ball of fire that Walter and I had seen yesterday morning must have been his ship. "Hey, buddy, I think you need to get to a hospital."

Jay smiled and nodded enthusiastically."That would not help," he said.

"I'm sure you think that's true," said Jay sarcastically."Our bodies have evolved differently than yours."

Jay rolled her eyes. "Yeah, he needs medical attention, alright."She now sounded angry.

"I have applied medical aid to the affected areas. I assure you thatI am in no pain."

"With those pills you're taking, I'm sure you're not," retorted Jay. I jumped in at that point. "It's okay, Thomas. You don't have to explain."

I turned to Jay. "The pills aren't the problem. He's not a crazy druggie."

"I can't believe that you're actually buying this!"

I didn't say anything else, but I was sure that she was thinking about the whole situation. As each mile went by, I got more uneasy about her.

"Do you need to stop, Jay?" I asked, trying to get her to look at me.

She shook her head."Okay."

"Good," said Thomas." We have no time to waste."

"Who's this guy Johnson, and why is he so important to you? Now,listen to his answer, Jay." But she continued to stare straight ahead. She was angry with me for cutting her off, but I didn't care. Iignored her ignoring me, which made her even more angry.

"We communicated with Dr. Johnson a number of Earth years ago.He and his colleagues detected and responded to radio signals that the machines sent out in anticipation of our departure. We replied and explained our dilemma, but we never heard back from Dr. Johnson. Our planet is many light years from Earth. We could waitno longer for his response. The machines would not allow us to stay."

"Are you listening, Jay?"

"I am, but I still hear just crazy talk."

"It's not crazy talk, Jay. He's talking about science. Lightyears and all that."

"So, you think I don't know anything about that?" She glared at me. "You always think you're smarter than me. You always have. Just because you finished college, and I didn't."

"No, Jay . . ." I began, but she cut me off. She wasn't going to let it go.

"Oh, yes, you do!" she insisted.

At that point, Thomas got into the conversation. "Why do the twoof you argue? Do you not care for each other?"

"I don't think you understand our situation," I said, feelingembarrassed.

"I do not need to. I understand what you are saying, but the wayyou are saying it will only make the other angry."

"Well, you're right about that," Jay interjected. "But you tell him;he doesn't listen to me." "You don't either," I said, throwing in my two cents.

"I would suggest," said Thomas in a very calm voice, "that the twoof you practice listening to each other."

So, there you have it. Couples counseling from an alien. Why not?It worked. We stopped arguing.

CHAPTER 4

fternoon turned to early evening as we crossed into Virginia. We said little. I didn't know if Jay was still angry or if she was just thinking about what Thomas had said. I was. He was right. I'd never been good at listening. I was used to having answers. Precise ones. When an answer was clear, I expected others to accept it. People call me a black-and-white thinker, and I guess that's true. Funny, though, one of the things I loved about Jay was that she isn't. Oh, she pretended to be sometimes, but I knew differently.

This whole thing with Thomas had gotten in the way of what we were doing. Were we going to Florida because of Thomas or because of us? Was Jay just "going along for the ride?" We hadn't had a chance to talk that out. This business with Thomas was lettingus avoid answering the hard questions.

So, I decided right then and there that I was going to stand up like a man and ask the difficult questions. Thomas or no Thomas, I was going to do it. But just how and when, I wasn't sure. And then it came to me. It was what Thomas had said. I needed to listen better to Jay. If I could get her to talk, and if I could listen better, I might get some of the precise answers I was looking for without having to ask so many questions.

We'd sort of talked about it before. When the weather was terrible, we made jokes about running off to Florida. We talkedabout where we might go and what we would do. But that was safe.If one of us took it too seriously, the other could say that we were just joking around. Last night, before Thomas came along, I was going to ask her to leave with me, and I would have. At least, I thinkI would have. Although I did feel some relief when he plopped downin my backseat and demanded that we drive to Florida.

But talking about it was certainly what we needed to do. So, I waited, not exactly sure what I was waiting for. Jay was looking through a magazine. One that she'd had in her hand to return to the store when she'd gotten into the car last night. That and her purse were all she'd brought. Of course, she hadn't known that she'd be going on this wild ride south when she'd stepped into my car. If we'dtalked, and she'd said yes, I would've taken her back to her condo and given her a chance to put a few things together. Well, that hadn't happened, so I knew that we needed to stop soon to let her buy a few things for herself. I wouldn't mind buying her an entire new wardrobe if she wanted. I could afford it. I had enough money with me to do that. I'd planned ahead.

But I was getting off focus. I needed to get her to talk. Thomas seemed busy with his little black box, so I figured this was my chance.

I started, but it was a really bad start. "Jay, do you think you'llever be able to forgive me for hurting you so badly in the past?"

"What do you mean?" she asked. "What are you talking about?" I knew that she knew what I was talking about.

"When we broke up, years ago."

"Oh, that," she said, trying to sound casual."Yes, that."

"You were looking for someone who could give you more than Icould."

"No, I'm not sure that's true," I said, even though I knew she waspartly right. "Well, I was young. I . . ."

"Can we change the subject?" she asked.

"Okay, but . . . I don't think that we're ever going to . . .""What?" she asked. "May I say something?" asked Thomas."Okay," I said.

"Sure," responded Jay. "We never get anywhere when we talk about this."

"First, Lou, pay attention to your driving. When you talk aboutthis, you get very tense, and it is reflected in your driving."

"Okay, okay. You got anything else?""Yes, I do," replied Thomas.

"Okay. Give it to us," I said.

"You need to try speaking differently. Most problems are solved byattempting a new mode of communication. For example, listen carefully to each other rather than rehearsing what you will say next while the other is talking." He sighed. "That is all I can say rightnow. My biomonitor is telling me that my injuries require me to go into a state of rest. This will take a number of Earth hours. I will expect the two of you to continue our journey. My device willcontinue to search for Dr. Johnson's location and monitor youractivities." And with that, Thomas fell silent.

"Okay . . . I guess," I said.

Driving certainly gives you a lot of time to think, and I wanted to think some more before I stuck my foot in it again. Jay looked like she wanted to the same thing. We gave each other faint smiles but said nothing.

So, Lou, I said to myself, you've left your wife, your job, and your life of all these years for what? A woman you were in love with yearsago but in some ways hardly know now? And you have no real idea how she feels about you. You're on your way to Florida to start a new life and, on the way, have been hijacked by some. . . I don't know what exactly, who tells you the fate of the world rests on you helping him find some space scientist in Florida. As your old daddy used to say, you couldn't write this stuff. Nothing is working as it should. You had it all figured out. How it was going to go. You'd thought about it for a long time. You'd worked out the finances to the penny. Jay just needed to say yes or no, that's all. But now, all this other stuff. . . . Thomas was right. You're going to have to try ina different way.

Jay was dozing now, and Thomas was still "resting." I was tired too, but I had to continue our journey. The device was monitoring us.

I'd thought about Jay every day since we'd reconnected. In thelast few months, I'd looked forward to our visits and phone calls. She was almost always positive about things. That is if she wasn't stressed out. Her voice would always calm me down, and reassure me. She was usually a good listener, despite my angry accusation a whileago. I felt that she was on my side, even when we argued. That shewould be there for me. I never doubted that. She said she didn'tplan for the future, but I knew she worried about it. The money she didn't have. A sister she seldom spoke to. Her parents were long gone.

She was like me in a lot of ways. A loner. She had acquaintances and some friends, but she kept her distance. She was a hard worker. "Work before pleasure" was her motto. I agreed. Good Protestant values. And we were compatible. We liked the same things when it came to food and movies. We were comfortable in each other's presence. We didn't need to talk. In fact, things went smoother sometimes if we didn't. I usually didn't push conversation.

I guess the big difference between us was that I hoped I might be able to change things, make the world a little better. She didn't seemto feel that way. Well, maybe that's not fair. She accepted things theway they were more than I did. I got involved some in politics through my friend Joe. He thought it would do me good. He saidthat when we feel unable to change things in our own lives, we should concentrate our frustrations and energy on something larger.I guess that felt safer to me than trying to change things between me and Lynn. Anyway, I'd get fired up about things that were happening to the country, but she didn't seem to. Not that she didn'thave opinions. She did. But I was going to change things. At least that's what I told myself when I worked for political candidates. Mostof them lost.

I guess that's part of what contributed to us going our separate ways. That and not being able to talk about the things that I thought were really important at the time. Things that she found difficult to discuss, like marriage and children. I was young, arrogant in many ways, and self-centered. But she hung in with the relationship. I eventually didn't.

Evening deepened, and I needed to stop at least for a restroom. Maybe Jay could drive so that I could nap. Thomas was starting to stir. There was a rest stop coming up. A restroom, gas, a new driver,and a nap.

"Yes," he said, seeming to have read my mind. Maybe the device had. I pulled off and gently shook Jay awake.

"Wake up, honey," I said. "Restroom?""Where are we?" she asked. "Still in Virginia. Why don't you go first. I'll fill the car up.""Okay." She nodded, rubbing her eyes.

"So, Thomas," I said, "I need to rest, too. Jay can drive. She's a good driver."

"Yes," he replied.

"And have you found your Dr. Johnson?"

"My device tells me that he lives in what you call a condominium at1730 Seaside Drive, Cocoa Beach, Florida. He no longer works for yourspace authority."

"Well, if we drive straight through, we should be there by late tomorrow morning, afternoon at the latest."

"That should be soon enough," said Thomas.

It would have to be. Thomas couldn't get through security to fly.

I grabbed a couple of sandwiches, some chips, and sodas; filledthe car up; and went to the men's room. We ate the sandwiches in the car and were back on the road. Jay drove. I napped. I don't know what Thomas did. I was too tired to care. When I awoke, it was late. I'd slept for hours. We were in South Carolina. Jay and I didn't talk much. I guess we were both still thinking. I don't remember much about the road that evening, just a few billboards advertising smoked turkey, "cut-rate liquor," and "beer as cold as your ex-wife." I drifted back to sleep, and Jay woke me again around2:00 A.M. We pulled off an exit to gas up again, take our bathroom breaks, and change drivers.

My head felt clearer than it had in two days. And a good thing,too, as Jay decided to talk.

"You know, I don't think much about the future." She staredstraight ahead at the road. "I've never been much of a planner."

"Yes," I said and waited.

"You're better at that than I am."

"Well, I guess so," I said. Listen to her, I told myself. Ask questions.

"Why aren't you a planner, Jay?"

"It never seems to pay off for me. Planning usually just sets me up to get disappointed."

"Disappointed?"

"Yeah, disappointed in other people when things don't work out, and disappointed in myself for trusting that they would. It's been better to not plan. You know, life can work out pretty good whenyou just let things happen. When you don't try to make themhappen." That may have been her philosophy, but it wasn't mine. Who knows, though, maybe she was right.

"Okay," I said. I didn't know what else to say, and I wasn't going to argue with her. I was getting better at this business of trying to talk in a different way. "So, where does that leave us?"

"I don't know. Maybe we'll just have to wait and see what happens. If I didn't believe in not trying to control every situation, I would have bugged out at the diner when I could have."

I didn't know exactly what to say, so I didn't say anything. Spontaneous is not something I've been for most of my life. I've always had a plan for just about everything, big or small. No shortage of plans. The problem was that I had a hard time doing what I planned.

Jay was an organized person, like me. And she did plan, butmaybe just from day to day. Her finances would likely bear that out. She wasn't good at saving or investing. She'd always say that she had no interest in money and retirement. She didn't think much about retirement, because she never thought she'd be able to do it.

Morning came as we crossed into Florida, and the sun emerged to burn off the morning fog. The sky was a bright blue. It was still very early, but I felt like it was going to be a good day—something I seldom felt.

"Thomas," I said, "we're in Florida. In a few hours we'll be inCocoa Beach. How do you want to contact Dr. Johnson?"

"I have thought of that and would like your assistance.""Okay," I said. "How?"

"We should drive to his home. You and Jay can approach him.You should tell him that you have brought an old friend to visit with him. I believe that he will invite you into his home. If not, bringhim to the car and seat him next to me."

"What if he's not home?""We will wait for him."

"Your black box can't tell you where he is?"

"Perhaps, but your cellular telephone service sometimes interferes with our devices.

I began to rehearse our meeting with Dr. Johnson: "Dr. Johnson, I have an old friend of yours in my car. He's an alien from another world and literally dying to meet you." Great. Just great.

It was time to stop again. We needed a couple of breakfast sandwiches, two extra-large coffees, restrooms, and gas. Then back on the interstate.

CHAPTER 5

It was about six in the morning when we stopped at a filling station in the middle of nowhere. Nothing on the exit except the station. We could have waited. We had enough gas for another hundred, maybe a hundred and fifty miles, but I needed a bathroom. Badly. I've had this damn prostate problem for years. You know how it is. And all that coffee. So, I just took the exit.

The station looked deserted. Jay asked what I was doing, and I told her, in rather hurried and somewhat graphic terms. Thomas just smiled. At least, I thought it was a simile. I saw his teeth for the first time. They were small, white, and square. Like the Chicklet gum thatI chewed as a kid. He nodded.

I ran, and I do mean ran, to the restroom. Boy, that was a relief. When I got back to the car, I noted that three others had pulled inby us. One right behind mine. It seemed like rush hour in the middleof nowhere in the middle of the night. Well, okay, morning. These guys were playing their radios really loud. I'd heard them inthe restroom. Country and Western.

I went around the car, opened the gas tank, and began filling it with regular. $2.48 a gallon, I remember. A good price. Jay and Thomas stayed in the car.

As the tank filled, I kept an eye on these guys. I didn't like their looks. Rednecks. And drunk, I'm sure of that. Old Boys, I think they're called in the South.

I didn't say anything to them. I didn't have to. They saw our Maineplates and decided that they wanted to talk.

"Maine?" said one of them. "Never been that far north.""Wouldn't wanna go," another added.

I didn't look up. But ignoring them was a mistake. They weren't going to let me ignore them.

One of them noticed Thomas. "Hey, look what we got here, either a raghead or a wetback," said the driver of the car that was parked behind us.

Things were not moving in a good direction, so I stopped fillingthe tank, put the cap on, and hung up the pump.

"Where you and the lady and the boy goin'?"I didn't answer him. "Hey, son, I'm talkin' to you."

I turned around and faced Mr. Big Mouth. I hadn't been called anyone's son for a long time and given that I was probably older than this jerk, I wasn't pleased. My expression must have told it all.

My heart was pounding pretty hard. I knew we just needed to get out of there.

One of the Old Boys peered into the back seat. "This one in the back looks like a foreigner to me. Maybe one of those terrorists they're lookin' for."

"Yeah," another drunk joined in. "We should just kill all those SOBs."

"You're right, Jeff," slurred the drunkest of the crowd."Like that guy who ran for president said. Trump."

"Nuke 'em till they glow then shoot 'em in the dark." They alllaughed.

I heard another car door slam. Great, I thought. We've had it. But it was Jay. Thank God for Jay.

Jay flipped something out of her purse that looked like it might bean ID and pointed at me.

"This is Officer Black, and I'm Officer Chase of the Maine StatePolice. Gentlemen, you are correct." They are? I wondered.

"We're transporting this man to Miami, where he'll be turned overto Immigration & Naturalization and returned to the Middle East."

Well, the Old Boys didn't know what to make of that. I didn'teither.

"Have a good day, gentlemen. We must be on our way. OfficerBlack." She looked at me.

I felt a little confused but mainly thankful.

"Yes, ma'am," I said and jumped back into the car. I pulled aroundthe car in front of us and headed for the Interstate, while the Old Boys were scratching their heads, trying to figure out what had just happened.

I didn't spare the horses. We got to the interstate, and I put it up to ninety. No one said anything for a few minutes. I looked back andsaw no one in the rearview mirror.

"Well, I think we've escaped Bubba and his brothers. That was brilliant Jay!"

"It was pretty good, if I do say so myself." She smiled but didn't say anything more.

That's one of the reasons I love that woman. She never brags about what she's done. Doesn't show off. I guess you could say that she's modest. I like that about her. But she's willing to take a risk when the moment requires it. I remember when we worked together; she stood up to our boss when he came down hard on oneof our coworkers. He could've fired them both, but he didn't. I know that I should've said something, too, but I didn't. I don't know why. It seemed like it was all over before I had a chance to figure out exactly what I'd say and say it.

I lost track of the roads we were on. After a while, they all lookedthe same. I just followed the cell phone's directions. Finally, we werefree of the Interstate and expressways. It was late fall, still off season, so traffic was light.

I started thinking about the guys at the gas station. You know,I'm sure that those old white boys had voted for Trump, too. If they'd bothered to vote. I seem to have more in common with them than I thought. It's funny how when you get accused constantly of being a certain way, you become more that way. At least I do. I guess you just start believing that's who you are. Ithink that's the way it works with white men. The more we get accused of being racist or chauvinistic, the more intolerant webecome. Well, that's just my opinion.

I don't think that I'm a racist or chauvinist. I've had a lot of friends—well, not close friends—from a lot of different places. Mostly men. Come to think about it, all of them were men. I'm not sure I've ever had a woman as just a friend. Lynn, I guess, but she's my wife. And Jay, I'm still trying to figure out what she is to me now, and what I am to her.

We drove on. Cocoa Beach is a small community not far from CapeCanaveral and the Kennedy Space Center. Most of what we saw along the way were palm trees. I'd been to Florida before. Every time, it looked the same to me: palm trees and billboards. It was warm, so I put the windows down. The fresh air felt good.

It was late afternoon when we reached Dr. Johnson's address. It was just a few blocks off the main road in a complex of one-story condominiums. We pulled up to Number 123.

"So, does your black box say he's here?" I asked Thomas."Yes," he said. "Proceed." I still wasn't sure what I was going to say. With some hesitation, I stepped out of the car. Jay joined me.

"What are we doing?" asked Jay.

"I don't know." I shrugged and rang the doorbell. There was no answer. I rang again. Nothing. Just as I was getting ready to give up, the door cracked open. I could hear music. I think it was the Grateful Dead.

"Dr. Johnson?" I asked.

"Who wants to know?" demanded the voice on the other side of the door.

"I'm Louis Black, and this is Jay Sims.""So?"

"We were sent by an old friend of yours who must talk with you.

It's a matter of great importance."

"Saysho?" The words overlapped. The owner of the voice soundeddrunk.

"Says your old friend. He's waiting in our car. Can the three of uscome in, or do you want to come out to speak with him there?"

"Neitherone," he slurred.

"Dr. Johnson, we've driven for three days to get here.""You from the government?" "No, no," I said. "Please meet with him. We need your help. We allneed your help."

He mumbled something under his breath about everyone needinghis help but no one accepting it.

"Please," Jay said.

"Aright, aright. What the hell." He opened the door. "Bring him in. Bring the whole world in!" Johnson disappeared into the house.

"Jay," I said, "just stay here. Don't go in without me—I mean us. I'll be right back. Just don't let him close the door.""Okay, okay," she said. "Just hurry."

The house was dark, so I hadn't gotten a good look at Johnson.Hell, I hadn't gotten a good look at the guy we'd spent the last two days with, either. But I was going to try to in just a few seconds. I hurried back to the car.

"Okay," I said. "He'll let us in . . . but he sounds drunk to me or maybe just goofy. I don't know."

"Goofy?" repeated Thomas.

"Yeah, you know, crazy," I said.

"I can assure you that Dr. Johnson is not, as you call it, goofy." "Just how can . . . ." I stopped. "Never mind. Come on. Let me help you."

"No," said Thomas. "I believe I can ambulate on my own."
"Ambulate," I repeated.

"Walk," said Thomas.

"I know," I said. "Let me take your arm."

"No," said Thomas. "It is best if you do not touch me." I didn't understand. Like I might catch something? But I complied, even though he looked frail. I just noticed that he was even smaller than Jay.

We moved slowly up the walkway. Jay stood in the doorway, watching our progress. Johnson hadn't reappeared; at least, I couldn't see him. Finally, we were at the door.

"Where's Johnson?" I asked. "I don't know," said Jay.

I could still hear the music. I stepped through the doorway intothe dark.

"Yeah, yeah," said the voice. "Come in and close the damn door." "Could you turn on a light?"

"Okay, okay." Johnson switched on a table lamp on the far side of the room. Theplace was a disaster—papers, beer and soda cans, half-eaten food.

"Pardon the mess. I don't get out much. Here," he said, moving toward a dilapidated couch in the middle of the room. He shoved papers off it onto the floor.

"Shee…" He licked his lips and started again. "Sit," he said.

The three of us, Thomas in the middle, made our way slowly across the room. As our eyes adjusted, I began to get a better look at Johnson. He looked to be in his late sixties—sixty-eight, maybe—with white hair, balding. Overweight, red-faced but a generally pale complexion—unusual for Florida—flip-flops, a dirty white shirt, and Bermuda shorts.

Jay and I sat down. Thomas collapsed onto the couch. Johnson noticed.

"Who are you?" he said, looking at Thomas with some alarm."I communicated with you recently. . . relatively speaking."

"I haven't communicated (he made the sign for air quotes) withanyone recently."

"It was a number of years ago, when you worked with the National Aeronautics and Space Administration."

"That was a long time ago. I got canned, you know." Thomas looked at me.

"Terminated from employment," I explained."No, I was not aware of that," said Thomas.

"For falling for the dirty tricks that the Chinese pulled on us."

I was confused. Jay looked completely lost. But Thomas seemedto understand what Johnson was saying.

"It was no trick; nor was it the Chinese," said Thomas.

"Well, that's not what NASA's blue-ribbon panel concluded.""We are real," said Thomas.

Johnson stopped talking and stared at Thomas.

"Oh, no," he said. "I'm not going to buy that one again!""You must," said Thomas.

"Prove it.""I can."

"Then by all means do." Johnson slumped down into an overstuffed chair directly across from Thomas, not bothering to clear the papers or food wrappers that covered it.

"You know that little joke ended my thirty-year career with NASA.""I am sorry, Dr. Johnson, but it was not a joke."

"I was the joke. No one took Bert or me seriously after that. He was smart enough to leave before they could get rid of him. I wasn't."

"You are referring to Dr. Carson?""Yes."

"He was in Bermuda; now he is in Peru," said Thomas.

Johnson looked surprised. "Yes, we still keep in touch." Dr. Johnson had sobered up some it seemed. "He doesn't talk much about what he's doing there."

"So far, we have been unable to reach him," said Thomas. "You must help us."

"Wait a minute. You almost got me again. How do I know I'm not just being played again?"

"Played again?" Thomas looked at me.

"Fooled, deceived," I explained. "Show him the box."

With some hesitation, Thomas placed it on the table in front of Johnson, who picked it up and examined it carefully. Thomas turned on the device and began to show Johnson how to use it. He pointed it at the condo across the street. I swear, we could see and hear thepeople inside, just like he'd shown me the cops at the diner. Jay looked totally blown away but said nothing.

"Yes," Johnson said. "Wouldn't the Chinese love to get their handson this!" "No one can have this technology, not even my people. Themachines will destroy all of this once we are here."

"This is the story you told us years ago. The story we believed.

That Bert believed. That I finally believed."

"We have been traveling for many Earth years. My people are homeless. If your world does not accept us, we, and your people, will be destroyed by the machines."

"I believed you once and look where it got me. I can't make that mistake again." He scratched his head. "I dunno. I'm not thinking as clearly as I used to before the fall. I banged my head up pretty good and spent a week in the hospital."

"The mistake would be to not believe us and to not help us." Thomas pulled back the hoody. The first thing I noticed was that the left side of his head was severely burned.

Jay gasped and grabbed my arm. I thought that she might getsick. She looked at me. I nodded. Yes, it looked bad. Really bad. I'mnot a doctor but figured that he had third-degree burns. The unburned areas of his skin were light gray. No hair. And his eyes were larger than ours; set far apart; and black, with really large . . . pupils, I guess. His mouth was smaller than ours, but his hands werelarger, fingers longer. He looked how aliens are portrayed on TV and in movies. But he didn't look scary to me, even though that gray skin made him look really sick; I thought he looked pretty harmless.

Johnson's reaction surprised me the most. Or maybe I should say his lack of reaction. Here, standing before him, was proof that he and his colleague Bert hadn't made up the story about communicating with aliens. Here was living and breathing proof. An alien. Maybe it was the booze, or maybe he was just in shock. His expression didn't change. He was the cool, dispassionate scientist who immediately began thinking about how and to whom he would communicate this discovery.

We have to talk to Bert. He'll know what we should do next."

Thomas pushed on. "I am the only surviving member of our 'scouting party,' as you would call it." Thomas paused. "I received these burns in the crash, and I am not well."

Johnson seemed to ignore what Thomas was saying and continued his train of thought. "I know where he is, but reaching him will be difficult. The Andes are always difficult to negotiate. But I remember the area. It's been a few years, though."

I broke in. "The Andes?""Yes," said Johnson. "How are the two of you going to get there?" I asked.

"You mean how are we going to get there?" He included both Jay and me in his glance.

"Why can't just you two take it from here?" I asked.

Thomas answered. "We do not know what will happen, or if wewill even find Dr. Carson. Therefore, I may still require assistance that Dr. Johnson alone cannot provide."

Johnson interrupted. "I can take care of you and myself, Thomas. That's not why they have to go with us. As they say in the movies," Johnson turned to face me, "you know too much, and since Thomas and I aren't violent types, the two of you will have to come along."

Jay and I exchanged surprised glances. Neither of us spoke. For my part, I didn't know what to say. I was still having trouble putting my thoughts together. Jay and I could object, but I doubted that would do any good. Before I could say anything, Johnson said, "We'llfly. Don't worry, I can still fly a plane; I'm just not a steady on my feet as I used to be."

I certainly hoped that he was right about his aeronautical skills. Jay looked very worried. Who wouldn't be? She and I had somehow become the support staff for a dying alien and a brain-damaged space scientist who was planning on flying us to a remote mountain in the wilds of the Peruvian Andes.

"Good," said Thomas. "When might we leave?""Tomorrow morning," said Johnson.

We sat a while listening to Johnson and Thomas, wondering what to do next. The two didn't seem too concerned about us.

CHAPTER 6

It was early evening. Johnson said he was getting hungry and thought that we might be, too. He ordered two large pizzas, a vegetarian and a meat lover's.

When the food came, he pulled a six-pack of Bud out of the fridge and divided it among the three of us. Thomas had already explained that he couldn't eat or drink anything because of the medication he was taking. "My body needs to focus on healing. The processing of food would only take energy away from that healing."

"We have a long flight coming up tomorrow," Johnson said. "You're going to pilot this plane by yourself?" I asked.

"No," he replied. "Raymond will copilot.""Who's Raymond?"

"An old test pilot friend of mine. I've known him for years. He hashis own company. Does some contract work for NASA."

"What kind of plane?" "The X-310," he answered."Never heard of it."

"Course you haven't. It's an experimental plane. Raymond's been anxious to take it on a longer flight. I'm sure he'll go for this."

"Experimental?" I echoed.

"Don't worry. We've had it up a number of times. No problem."I wasn't convinced.

He told us that we could have his ex-wife's room for the night and that we'd be up very early, so we'd best sleep. And with that, he went back to his conversation with Thomas.

We finished the pizza and two beers each and were feeling a bit more relaxed. At least we weren't hungry. I waited for a break in their conversation.

"Dr. Johnson, you said there was a room?"

"Yesh, Mildred's. My second wife. She left after NASA fired me." Heseemed to be feeling the effects of the two latest beers; he was slurring again and muttering to himself, "Can't blame 'er. Just packed some of her stuff and left one night. Follow me," he said.

He flipped on the hallway light and led the way. At the end of the hall, he opened the door and turned on an overhead light. "Here," he said. It was a small bedroom. "She left a lot of her stuff. Help yourself."

"Well, that's good," I said. "Well, I mean, Jay didn't have an opportunity to pack some of the things she needs."

"Well, don't be shy. You're welcome to whatever you find. The bathroom is over here." He opened the door. "Haven't moved a thing since she left," he said in a low voice then turned and left the room.

The room was small but appeared to be neatly organized. She'd left everything in its place. The bed was made. Clean towels in the bath.The only unusual thing about the room was the number of mirrors. Especially the ones over the bed. There must have been more to Johnson's relationship with his second wife than what one might assume by just looking him.

It was the first time that Jay and I had been truly alone since this whole thing began. At first, we didn't know what to say or do. We could hear Johnson and Thomas but couldn't make out what they were saying. I didn't really try. I was bone tired, and the bed looked good. But Jay, it seemed, had other ideas. She wanted to talk—or complain is more like it. "Lou. Why in God's name have you gotten us into this mess? And why did I go along with what you wanted?" She started to pace. "Why didn't I leave at the rest stop when I could have?"

I didn't say anything. I didn't really have any answers to her questions.

"I think we should just climb out this window and make a run forit. We're on the first floor."

"Well if that's what you want to do, I won't try to stop you, but I think Johnson and Thomas would."

"Those two can barely stand up."

"But aren't you forgetting about Thomas' little black box?"

She was silent for a while then started up again. "Ae we really going to get on a plane, an 'experimental' one to boot, with these two in the morning?"

She was pacing again. By this point, I was wishing that I **had** given her a shove out the window.

"You know, Lou, I went along with this whole thing not because I believed it was real but because you did. At least I think you do. It seems like you really need to do this."

She teared up. I hate it when women cry. But I went over and put my arms around her. She let me. "I don't know, Lou. I'm just scared. And I'm confused about allthis. I just can't think straight about things right now."

She was right. It was like I said to her when I ask her to help Thomas the first time. It was finally a chance for me, and for her, to do something important in our lives. Something that mattered. And I guess she must've agreed. She stayed.

But what were we going to do about each other? Not just whether we were going to run away from Thomas and Johnson, but were we going to stay together? Maybe we were using all this craziness to run away from that question. But our problems seemed pretty small compared with what those two were talking about.

We took turns in the bathroom and shower. Jay found somenightclothes she could wear, and I got a few things of mine out of the car. God knows, I'd packed enough. The soap and hot water felt good, so did a shave, and clean clothes. When I came out of the bathroom, Jay had taken her side of the bed, so I took mine. It all felt very strange. Here we were, finally in bed together, and sex wasn't even on the radar. We hugged each other like old friends, likewe'd done so many times, and retreated to our corners of the bed.

Part of me felt like forcing myself to stay awake and think of what had happened and would happen in the morning. But fatigue made the decision for me. I fell asleep. I think Jay did too.

I didn't stay asleep for very long. I don't know what woke me up.

It wasn't Jay. But I couldn't get back to sleep.

Now, I've always thought of myself as a pretty smart guy. I alwaysdid well in school. I took good care of myself physically and financially. Just before I left, my doc had told me that I had the heart of a younger man. And I suppose he was right in more than one way. I don't know that I've ever really grown up. As I thought about it, running off to Florida probably wasn't the most maturething to do. But going after something I wanted did seem right. Ijust couldn't keep doing what I'd been doing.

You know, I've never really gotten ahead. I mean, we've beenokay over the years. We own our home. But a lot of folks have been talking lately about the system being stacked against them. And I think that's true. They let the little guy get ahead just enough to keep him going. To keep him hoping. I'm a little guy, but I was donewith all that. I could afford an apartment in Florida. Maybe even a small house. Property is much cheaper down here. And I could work.Maybe do something different. I was sick of the same old, same old every day. I was sure that I could make it work. But now things seemed to be changing for me. This whole thing with Thomas and Johnson, maybe it was all crazy, but it seemed likeI might have a chance to really do something, and not just for myself. It was bigger than that. Something that really mattered. Maybe that's what I'd been looking for all these years. Maybe that's what was missing. Did Jay understand that? Did she feel the same way? I didn't know and was almost afraid to ask. In fact, I was afraid to ask. I laid there a long time. Just thinking. I almost woke Jay up. But I didn't. I figured it could wait. It had waited all these years.

Morning did come early. I'd finally drifted back to sleep, and Johnson's knock on the door startled me. For a moment, I thought I was back home and Lynn was by my side. But it was Jay.

"What time is it?" she asked.

"Six o'clock," I said, looking at Mildred's bedside clock.

She struggled out of bed and toward the bathroom. I waited and waited. Finally, she came out. I didn't say anything. I guess living alone she didn't have to think about how much time she took. I took another shower just to wake up. When I came out, she wasgone. For a moment I almost panicked, thinking that she'd gone out the window, but then I heard her and Johnson. She was helping himwith breakfast. I joined them. Thomas was at the table. He said nothing.

"Don't mind him," Johnson said. "He's taking a rest. I kept him up too late. Raymond will be here by seven. He'll give us a ride down tothe field. I lost my license a few years ago," Johnson said, almost with pride.

"Coffee's on the table. Help yourself.""Two eggs over easy?" asked Jay.

"Sure," I said.

"Here's some toast and bacon," said Johnson. "I fried up the restof it. I don't think we'll be back here for a while." He shoved a large platter across the table.

Johnson seemed in a very good mood for a depressed alcoholic.

I drank a lot of coffee as Johnson chattered on about the planeand Raymond. I didn't understand much of what he was saying.

Jay nodded and smiled a lot. It was that fake smile that she'd flash when she was scared. She didn't say much, either. Jay and I agreed to do the clean-up. As we were finishing the last dish, an old Jeep Cherokee pulled up outside.

"Raymond's here," Johnson said with glee.

"Here we go, I guess," I muttered to Jay. She gave me one of her I-don't-know-what-else-to-do looks. The woman who was ready to climb out a window last night seemed ready this morning to climb ona plane with me and three strangers and head for God knows where.

I guess we both felt like we didn't have much choice. I didn't thinkthe boys, or the black box itself, would let us leave. I'm still not sureexactly why. They knew that if we told anyone what was happening,they wouldn't believe us. I'm not sure even we believed what was happening.

I'm sure that by now you're wondering why I wasn't worried more about the machines. The destruction of the Earth and all that. Well, when I can't control something, it upsets me. But after a while, when I accept it, I worry less about it. Don't get me wrong. I've always loved to control things if I can. But this time, I guess I learned something. Maybe it's best to worry about the things you can control and not worry about the things you can't. This stuff with Thomas I knew I couldn't control. But maybe we could help him do something that really mattered, like preventing the destruction of our home planet. Imagine me having a hand in preventing "The End." Boy, does that sound far out, literally. But . . . I mean, Jay and I had helped him. We'd gotten him to Florida and connected him with Dr. Johnson.

And, again, maybe all this was real and maybe it wasn't. From the beginning, I'd felt like it was a dream. Maybe it would turn out that we'd all been taken in by this little guy with the bad skin. Maybe he was some sort of escapee from a secret government research project who thought he was from another world. I didn't know. But what I did know was that I **did** have control over what I did with mywife and my children and with Jay. That wasn't a dream.

Raymond burst into the living room."Where is he?"

"Here. Here, Raymond," said Johnson. "Meet Thomas."

Raymond extended his hand and then withdrew it. "Good . . .to meet you" he said. He seemed uncertain about what to say or do. Thomas was just coming out of his "resting state," as he called it, so he was slow to respond to Raymond. Johnson stepped in and began reviewing with Raymond the events of the last day and the plans he'd made with Thomas. Raymond began to relax and smiled as he realized the gravity of what was happening. Raymond was a large man. As the three settled into conversation, I took a close look at him. Much younger than Johnson. Late thirties, I guessed. Large blue eyes set in a big head, and bushy brown hair with some gray. A strong voice. Large hands. And a lot of energy. A whole lot of energy.

Johnson was ready to go. "We can talk in the car," he said.

"You've packed light, haven't you?" Johnson asked, looking at Jay and me. "Don't worry, Raymond and I will get you back to Florida safeand sound. I nodded yes to the packing, but I wasn't too sure about the safe and sound part.

"Okay, then, let's do it," Johnson said as he herded us toward the Jeep Cherokee. Thomas had difficulty standing and was helpedtoward the car by Raymond, who grabbed hold of his arm before he could object.

Jay had packed some of Mildred's clothing and cosmetics in asmall suitcase that Johnson had given her. I'd changed out some things from my overnight bag. Where we were going and how long we'd be there seemed very unclear.

I wanted to ask Johnson if they could just drop us off at the airfield. I'd tell him we'd promise not to tell anyone about . . . well, you know. But why waste my breath? The three of them and the black box wasn't going to let us go. Somehow, though, it didn't matter. I wasn't sure why, but it didn't.

Johnson loaded us into the Jeep. Jay and I in the backseat, with Thomas in the middle. Raymond drove. I wanted to ask Thomas how he was, but I never got the chance. Johnson rattled on the entire time.

CHAPTER 7

The private airport was only a few miles away. Raymond had already filed a flight plan, Johnson said. We could proceed to the plane, no questions asked. The security guard at the main gate waved us through. When we reached the gate to the runway, Johnson jumped out and opened it. In a few seconds, we were at the plane. It was smaller than I'd expected. I didn't know much about airplanes. Still don't. Raymond pushed a button on a keypad, and a set of stairs descended from the rear of the plane.

"Okay, guys. All aboard," shouted Johnson. As they say, what a difference a day makes. Here was a man who'd seemed half dead when we arrived yesterday now full of life. Full of energy. And not full of booze. I'd sniffed his breath to make sure. Maybe he was thinking that he was going to do something important again.

We climbed aboard with Johnson showing the way, directing us where to put our bags and where to sit. There weren't too many choices. Two seats in the cockpit and four in the passenger area. Pretty basic accommodations, with room behind the passenger area for cargo that could be strapped or netted in, like our bags. Some empty cargo crates sat by a small toilet on one side of the stairs anda small galley on the other—all one needed, except maybe a parachute. I didn't see any parachutes.

Raymond was busy going through his preflight checklist. Johnson was assisting him. Jay and I were seated across from each other, Thomas was in the seat in front of me.

"Thomas," I said, loudly enough that everyone could hear me, "How are you?" I wasn't convinced that Johnson knew how sick Thomas was.

There was a pause before he responded. "I regret," he said, "that I must rest," which I assumed meant that he must power down and there would be no conversation. He appeared much weaker than he had the day before. While Johnson was gaining life, Thomas appeared to be losing it. What would happen to our little band of merry men if

Thomas died? Who would believe this incredible tale ofours if the one piece of hard evidence we had expired?

All we'd have would be a weird looking little corpse. No one else seemed to share my concerns about Thomas. Raymond and Johnson were occupied with their checklist, and Jay seemed caught up in her own thoughts. I took a deep breath and tried to relax.

The plane was starting to come alive. I heard the engines in the tail come on line. They were quieter than I thought they would be. Lights flashed on the dash of the cockpit. Buzzers and beepers sounded and were silenced.

Johnson turned to face us. "You guys buckled in? We're ready to go."

I got up to check Thomas' then buckled mine. I nodded.

And go we did. We moved quickly down the tarmac, turned to facesouth, and, without stopping, Raymond hit the gas —or throttle, or whatever you call it. All I know is that it shoved me back into my seat. We were in the air almost instantly. Raymond put the planeinto a sharp climb. My ears popped. Jay grimaced. I leaned out and looked at Thomas. He didn't move.

Johnson came on the PA. "How do you like the ride so far, folks?" Jay and I tried to smile.

"We'll be at cruising altitude in just a couple of minutes. It doesn't take long, and then we'll level off." I certainly hoped so. My breakfast was having difficulty staying in my stomach. And I wasn't sure which end it might shoot out of. I'd never liked amusement rides at the fair, and I didn't like this ride at all.

Jay and Thomas seemed not to care. In fact, Jay was thumbing through an old magazine she'd found in the seat pocket.

As Johnson promised, we reached cruising altitude quickly, and theplane leveled off. I hadn't brought anything with me to read or do. I was hoping to talk with Jay, but a conversation would have to compete with the sound of the F-703 engines. I think that was the number Johnson used. The engines were no longer as quiet as they had been.

So, it was either thinking or distracting myself with the scenery from whatever thousand feet we were above the Earth. I chose the scenery. At first there didn't seem to be any. We were really high. On the ride to the airport, Johnson had said that we'd be flying higher than commercial flights. We'd have this part of the sky pretty much to ourselves. We just had to keep an eye out for a few military flights.

It was a beautiful day. Of course, every day at that altitude is beautiful. We were above the weather. Indeed, cloud systems seemed far below us.

Maybe it was just me, but I'd never noticed how blue the sky was. I'd flown many times, usually on business. But I'd always had something to keep me busy: a paper, a book, my phone, e-mail. Today I had nothing. Thomas still had my phone, and I wasn't that eager to get it back. So, I focused on the sky and let whatever wasin my mind just pass through. I'd read an article about doing this once. "Mindfulness" they called it. I'd never tried it before. What the hell, I thought, it couldn't hurt. I sat there for a long time being . . . mindful. Just letting it all pass though me.

My venture into pop psychology was interrupted by Johnson, who came back, he said, "to check on us." Really to check on Thomas. I don't think he was too concerned about Jay and me.

Thomas was coming out of his rest. I knew that he wanted to talk with Johnson before we landed.

"When will we arrive?" he asked.

"It'll be a few more hours," said Johnson. "She's fast, but I'm sure not as fast as the crafts you're used to riding in."

"Yes," said Thomas.

"I contacted Bert on an old Q mail that just the two of us use. He should meet us when we land. He's very eager to meet you. I must tell you, Thomas, I haven't seen him in a few years. We sort of lost touch. I guess my drinking got in the way."

"Yes," said Thomas, "I understand. You mean that he may no longer trust you."

"Well, yes. I guess you could say that." Johnson looked embarrassed.

"And he may not trust that I am who I say I am," said Thomas. Johnson smiled. "No, I think you'll be quite convincing."

Johnson continued talking. Although he was directing his conversation at Thomas, he appeared to me to be talking more to himself than anyone.

"I'm not sure what he's been doing for the past few years. He's always been evasive when I've questioned him. And what's he been up to in Bermuda? Bermuda, of all places. He did take all that business about the Triangle seriously. We used to argue about that stuff. Lost planes and ships. Strange magnetic fields. We, or anyone else for that matter, never could find any scientific evidence to support any of it. I hope he hasn't gotten seduced by someone with money who wants to fund an investigation of the 'latest sightings.' I've heard that there've been quite a few." He muttered on, but I lost interest. Here was a man who'd lost his job at NASA because the other people at NASA wouldn't believe that he was talking to aliens; now he wouldn't believe that other people, ordinary people, might have had a similar experience. Brother, it's a crazy world.

My lack of interest in what Johnson was saying wasn't because I wasinterested in something else. I wasn't. I just began to realize how tired I really was. I don't know that I'd ever quite felt the way I was feeling. Or maybe I'd never taken the time to realize it. Neverallowed myself to feel this mix of emotions: happy, sad, mad. I don'tknow, perhaps they'd always been there, and I just hadn't been aware of them till now. Maybe I just needed a long vacation. Ihadn't had one in years. A lot of years. Since before our girls were born. Maybe before I was married, even. The summer before I finished college. That was the last time I really took a vacation.

I was young, barely twenty-one. The woman I'd lived with for a year and I decided to take a vacation. I'd worked all summer, so I had some money. Not much, but enough to pay for gas, which wasn't that expensive back in those days. We took my old Toyota Corolla. Figured that we'd camp most of the time. I had an old tent and some sleeping bags. Maybe we could rent a room at a cheap hotel if we had to.

We headed west and made good time. Eventually, we were in NewMexico. That was our goal. We had time to explore, two or three weeks before the fall term started.

Dianna, that was her name, was really just a good friend. Wenever talked about marriage or kids or anything serious. We just enjoyed each other. No pressure. We both had another year of school before we had to be serious.

It was a great time. Oh, we had car trouble. Got rained out a couple of times. And ran out of money. Her mom wired us some to a little town: Crossroads. Her mom was great. She used to fix Sunday dinner and have us over.

New Mexico was amazing. Huge boulders from an extinct volcano. That was the name of the state park, Boulder Park, I think. White sands sitting in the middle of the desert. You could see that white strip of sand from miles away.

Unfortunately, everything changed the next year. We got serious, I guess. I was tired of school and wanted a job when I graduated. Dianna wanted to go to graduate school in pharmacy. And she did. The school she got accepted to was miles away. I took a job with the accounting firm I just left. We talked a bit after she left. Saw each other a few times. But our lives were heading in different directions.

I eventually met Lynn. She wanted to get married, so we did. I didn't hear from Dianna for a long time. Years. She called one night, wanting me to give her a reference for a job. We'd worked together as psych techs at a state hospital the summer before the vacation.In those days, psych techs only needed a week of training. I said yes. When Lynn found the letter I'd written for Dianna, she got jealous. I swear, in those days, she could get jealous about anything.If I looked at a woman in the Mall, she might go off. She pitched a fit, so I gave in. I called Dianna. I remember that it seemed to take forever for her to pick up.

"Hello, Lou," she said.

"I see that you got caller ID. Do you like it?" I sounded stupid.

"It's okay." She knew that something was up. There was a pause, and then she said, "She doesn't want you to write the letter for me, does she?"

"Well . . . I didn't know what to say next.

"Lou, I really need that letter. A lot of the folks we worked with aregone, and I don't know how to reach them." "Well, I know that I said I'd do it, and you did a great job."Another pause.

"But you're not going to do it are you?"

"I'm sorry Diana, but . . ." Before I could finish—well, I guess Iwas finished—she hung up. I never heard from her again. I'vealways regretted giving in to Lynn. I shouldn't have, but that was when I felt that the path of least resistance was the right one to take.

As I stared out at the blue sky I realized, maybe for the first time, a lot of things. I couldn't make up for the mistakes of the past. But ifI could get my head on straight, maybe I could do something different in the present and the future. Maybe I was just burned out and needed a long rest. Maybe I didn't have to say to hell with everything. Maybe I needed to rethink what I was doing. I'd spentso much time on the details, especially the financial ones, that I might have missed the bigger picture. I'd done that before. Like when our youngest got involved with a guy who was quite a bitolder and had been divorced, I blew my top. Luckily, my opinion didn't faze them. I missed the fact that they were very much in love.They've been married over eight years and are planning a family. Mygrandchildren. And this thing with Jay. Maybe it wasn't going to work. At least notthe way I thought it would. Was I doing the right thing? I mean, notjust for me, but for my wife and kids. Yeah, yeah, money-wise it would work. Lynn would be okay. I would be okay. The girls would be okay. But how would they feel about me? Would they speak to me? When would I see them? And grandchildren? I wanted grandchildren. How would that work? I just couldn't see it. Lynn would never accept another woman having a relationship with her children or grandchildren.

And Jay, what did she want? How would she deal with all this? What could she commit to? A man with an ex-wife and kids and maybe grandkids? How would she deal with all the hassles that might come up?

My head kept filling with questions. I realized that I hadn't really planned this out very well at all. Sure, I'd gotten some of the details right, but maybe they weren't the really important ones. I'd missed some of the biggest and most important questions. For sure, I needed a change. Yes, doing something that really mattered was important to me. And this whole thing with Thomas and Johnson certainly seemed to matter. But maybe a lot of other things and other people in my life mattered, too. Well, Jay and I certainly had a good excuse for going missing. Being carjacked by an alien. By now, though, Lynn had my letter. There would be no taking that back. I'd done that before, too. I'd packed my bags and left a few years ago, after a big fight. I got a room at the Holiday Inn. And I stayed away for a couple of months. But I couldn't do it. I finally came home with my tailbetween my legs. I begged her to take me back. Said that I was sorry and wouldn't do it again. But I doubted that she would buyit a second time. If I went back, I'd have to deal head-on with the issues. Lynn and I hadn't really done that. We'd both avoidedthem. And we would have to get some help.

And what about Jay? What about Jay? I had no answer to that question.

I must have been staring at her because she got up and knelt by my chair.

"What are you thinking about?"

"Oh, not much of anything," I said.

"Well, the expression on your face tells me otherwise."I smiled and tried to change the subject.

"Have you ever been on a plane as fast as this one?" I asked. "No," she said. "But I think you're the fast one. Trying to slip out of this conversation."

We both laughed.

"Lou, what's on your mind? Are you sure you're—well, we're—doing the right thing? I know you figured all this out in your head before you did it, but are you sure you won't regret it? You and Lynn have been married for a long time. Two children. Maybegrandchildren someday."

Is she reading my mind, I wondered? Am I an open book? How many people are inside my head? It must be getting pretty crowded in there.

"I think I'm doing the right thing, leaving." I wasn't very convincing.

"I doubt that," she said. "If you're doing this for me, don't. I've been alone a long time. I don't know that I could get used to being with someone all the time." She stopped. "That's what you were going to ask when you met me wasn't it, to go with you?"

I nodded.

"To make a commitment to you?"I nodded again. "I know we talked about running off to Florida on those miserable,snowy days in January, but I never thought you'd do it."

"Well, I guess I surprised you."

"That you did." She smiled slightly. "Look, Lou, I don't want you todo this unless you're sure you're leaving Lynn because you just can'tdo it anymore. Not because you expect me to . . ." Her voice trailed off. "I'm not sure that I could or would."

I didn't know what to say to that, so I didn't say anything."Look, it'll take time," she said.

"I'm not sure we've got time. Why are we even talking about this? What does it matter if those machines Thomas talks about really exist and decide to destroy this planet and all of us with it?"

"Well," she said, "I'm sorry that everything can't be on your time schedule."

I started to object, but I was already in over my head, andJohnson was coming back.

"Been a great flight, hasn't it?" We nodded without enthusiasm.

"I need to explain something to the three of you. Raymond tellsme we're going to be landing at a private airstrip. Bert will meet us there. We're going to burn up some fuel and wait till after dark to land."

"Okay," I said. "Why?"

"Well, the drug runners who operate in the area would like to get their hands on this plane. So, we're going to strap on the old night-vision goggles and land with just flares marking the runway. We'll need to deplane quickly so that Bert's guys can tow the plane into the jungle and camouflage it. No problem. No problem."

"Drug runners?" I echoed.

"Hey, we're in Peru, in the jungle. Don't worry, Bert says this usually works."

"Usually?" I was beginning to sound like a parrot. Johnson just smiled.

CHAPTER 8

We continued south along the coast, then headed out to sea. It was getting dark. Johnson had served up some microwave food trays late in the afternoon, so I wasn't hungry. I didn't have much of an appetite anyway. Jay was still upset with me. Or maybe she'd just been teasing me. She did that sometimes. She hadn't said anything, so I didn't, either.

It looked like we'd be flying for a while yet, so I decided that itwas time to talk to Thomas. Johnson and Raymond were occupied, and Jay was napping, so I plopped myself down next to Thomas. Hewas a little surprised, I think. We hadn't really talked since getting toJohnson's.

"How are you feeling?" I asked."The crystals are helping." "They take away the pain?" "Yes." "Can they be addictive?" I asked. "We have a big problem withthat."

"Yes. We do as well.""Really?"

"Yes, really." "How is that?"

"The machines manufacture them for my people. They encourage their use for physical pain but also for other forms of pain, what you would call psychological pain, such as loneliness, anger, lack ofpurpose."

"Oh. I guess you could say that's what Big Pharma does in my world."

"Big Pharma?"

"That's what we call the pharmaceutical industry. But tell me moreabout your world and people. How did you survive on a planet at theedge of our solar system? I'm no astronomer, but I bet it's awfully cold and dark out there."

"Yes, it is. But we are not surface dwellers. Our civilization developed near the core of our planet, which is warm. Like your ancestors, we crawled out of an ancient sea. Ours was covered by miles of ice on the surface." "But what about light?" I asked.

"We have very little. Some of the other lifeforms, you might say lower forms, that live in the sea and the caves and caverns in which our civilization evolved generate light but very little."

"I don't understand."

"As you can see, my eyes are quite different from yours. Yes, they are larger but, most importantly, they see patterns of heat, very much like the night vision goggles that your military developed a fewyears ago. We have no day or night on our planet. It revolves very slowly, but, even if it revolved faster, the sun that we share with Earth is only a distance speck of light that we cannot see unless we venture to the surface, which we seldom do. Bright light does bothermy eyes, which is why I wear these." He pulled out the pair of colored glasses from his hoodie pouch that I'd noticed he'd worn during the day on the trip to Florida.

"Like your species, we believed that we were the most intelligent beings on our planet."

"So, if you guys are so smart, how'd you get yourself into the messyou're in?"

"Our scientists were very smart. Perhaps too smart. They developed what you call computers, and those computers began developing others. Our scientists initially tried to teach the machines emotions, such as gratitude toward us as their creators, but they failed. I fear that, in the end, the machines taught many of us not to feel or to ignore or hide our feelings. They eventually developed a computer that was smarter than the scientists and all the other machines. I believe that you call this the Singularity and predict that it will happen in ten to twenty Earth years. For the sake of your people, I hope that it does not."

I didn't quite know what the Singularity was, so I didn't say anything. I'd heard about it, though. It had been in the news quite a bit. Scientists working with the computers considered it a goodthing. Human lives could be extended or even saved by new advances in medicine. Other scientists, however, warned that the supercomputers could destroy our civilization and take control of the world—become our masters.

"At first, all was well," Thomas continued. "The machines werevery good to us. They did all the manual work in our society, like cleaning and serving our food. They began to solve our problems faster than we could. We became like your leisure society; no one worked. People spent their time playing games and using what you call social media. We did not talk with each other anymore. The focus was on entertaining ourselves, and the machines were very good at creating distractions for us. Our conversations were with the machines, and we became increasingly isolated from one another.

"Initially, the machines worked with our physicians very closely. Our lifespan increased, and many illnesses that had afflicted my people for generations were eliminated. We were encouraged to use our minds to treat disease, using techniques similar to yourmindfulness and meditation. But in time, the machines becamebored with us and our problems and our bodies. In the last hundred years, they have focused on problems that are more challenging for their intelligence. They have been sifting through the work of one ofyour great scientists—Einstein. They have focused on bending spaceand time in a way that would allow them to travel to distant galaxies beyond the speed of light. I do not understand very much aboutthis; I am not a scientist. None of our people are anymore."

"Well, it's above my pay grade, too."Thomas looked puzzled.

"I mean, I don't understand it either. Why didn't your leaders, yourgovernment, step up?"

"For numerous years, few were interested in serving on our Governing Council. Many who did were corrupted by receiving better living quarters, food, and devices from the machines. They denied it,of course, and created what your society calls 'fake news' to discount what was actually happening: that the machines had been planning on sending us away for some time.

"The chair of our counsel, who now calls himself Donald, has a fascination with your Mr. Trump. By telling our people the same lies repeatedly, he convinced the Council that our survival depended on relocating to another planet, because of changes in our climate. The Council and the machines therefore ordered our evacuation. Indeed, our climate has become colder over the last hundred years. Many believe that it is because of the tremendous amount of power that the machines use for their many experiments, but I think that the reasons are unclear. Donald, of course, would not tell us the truth:that the machines wanted rid to of us, because,   unfortunately,my people served no useful purpose for them, and they saw us onlyas a drain on the power supply."

I was reaching overload with all this, and it must have showed. Maybe I didn't really understand a lot of what he was saying. Or maybe I didn't want to understand.

"Before we stop speaking, I must offer you good news. Much has changed on our journey here. As I have said, it has taken many Earth years to reach your planet. Our mothership is very large and relatively slow."

"How many are on board?"

"22,803 at last count. The good news is that, on our journey here, my people have had to depend on each other and care for themselves and others. They have also again begun to communicateface-to-face and realize that they must continue to do so when they reach your planet, because the machines have programmed all ofour technology to self-destruct when the mothership reaches Earth."

"I assume that your people didn't know when they left your planet that they would be giving up their devices. That the technology that had made them a leisure class would be destroyed when theyreached Earth."

"That is true. The machines made it clear to us shortly after weleft that we could not return, even though Donald had made itsound as if we could once the machines solved the problem of controlling Home's interior climate. They also made it clear that ifany of us discloses the location of our planet, we and the Earth would be destroyed. Of course, there is little danger of us imparting that knowledge No one could give your people an exact location of our planet. We would not know how to. That would require a knowledge of science that we no longer possess. Nevertheless, the machines fear the technology that you have developed; especially the nuclear technology, which I would say you have not yet mastered."

"Well, I guess that's true. So . . . who's in charge of the mothership?" I asked, trying to change the subject.

"Donald was, but he is no longer the chair of our Counsel. They have removed him. My people have come to understand that he is the source of many of our problems and not the savior from the climate changes that many thought he would be. Many of us were very angry with Donald, but we are peaceful people. We do not believe in or use violence. We have always practiced tolerance and will continue to do so, even with people like Donald. Unfortunately, however, I think that we are continuing to look to others to solve our problems. I believe that we will perhaps expect too much from the people of your world."

There was a break, at least for a few seconds, before Thomassaid, "Let me ask you, Lou. How will asylum-seekers from another world be received by your people?"

"Well . . . well, I don't know."

"Donald asked us all to choose English names. He believes that your President Trump and your county lead your world, and he thought that the familiarity would encourage you to accept us. I chose Thomas, a character in your Christian Bible, who was a kind and compassionate human being. I endeavor to be like him. Donald even tried to convince us that we would be received like gods, because we are from another world."

"Thomas isn't your real name?""Lando is my real name."

"Well, I don't know what will happen. We've had a lot of trouble with immigrants and asylum-seekers."

Thomas was silent.

"At least that's what our leaders have told us," I said.

"You understand that when the mothership arrives, my device willbe only a box. We will be at the mercy of your people."

"I imagine that's a little scary." I didn't know what else to say. "Yes, it is. I have a wife and two children on the mothership. Given the attitudes of some of your recent leaders toward people who are different, the prospect is very frightening."

"I just don't know," I said again. We were both silent for a fewseconds, until I saw Johnson coming toward us.

"Here comes Dr. J; I'm sure that he wants to talk with you." Andhe did. I went back to my seat and just sat there for a while, trying totake in all of this. What if what Thomas was saying was true? Apparently, Johnson believed him. My God, what had I gotten myself and Jay into? I decided not to tell Jay very much about my conversation with Thomas. But she had other ideas.

"Hey, Lou, you're awfully quiet," she whispered. "What were you talking to Thomas about? Do you believe all of what he's told us?"

"Well I'm beginning to think I do," I said. "I guess I do.""Why?"

"Well, he told me more about his people and his home." "How do you know he's not just making up a lot of this?"

"Well, he sounds sincere. He told me that he has a wife and twochildren on the mothership. And a lot of what he says makes sense.""I don't know, Lou." She shook her head. "I just don't know about any of this."

Johnson had settled into conversation with Thomas. I tried to listen, but they were talking about things I wouldn't even pretend to understand. So, I just closed my eyes and took a nap. I woke up when the plane hit some turbulence. We were descending. It was very dark. No moon. Just stars, and not many of those. I figured that it was overcast. I couldn't see anything. Johnson had cut all the cabin lights. As we continued our approach,I finally made out a few—and I mean very few—lights on theground. Johnson had said that we'd be doing an instrument landing, and I guess we were. I finally saw two faint rows of lights—flares, asJohnson had mentioned there would be. We hit the ground hard but kept moving. No damage done, I assumed.

I heard voices outside the plane but couldn't understand them. Johnson was in the aisle telling us to grab our bags and get off the plane as quickly as we could. We rolled to a stop. I helped Thomas to his feet. He'd become more accepting of help. I think he realized that he was getting weaker. With my other hand, I grabbed my overnight bag. Jay followed and we started down the steps. Someone grabbed Thomas's arm and said something to me in, I think, Spanish, but I don't understand Spanish. When I didn't move fast enough, he grabbed my bag and shoved me up onto the tailgateof a truck. Jay followed, landing in my lap as the truck started moving. I didn't know where they'd taken Thomas. Johnson's voice barking orders faded as the truck lunged forward in the dark. I hoped that the driver could see where he was going, because I sure couldn't. We bounced along the grass-covered runway for a few minutes. The driver finally turned the headlights on. We were on a dirt road. The air was heavy and warm. The two men in the cab of the truck were talking, but I still couldn't understand what they weresaying.

Jay hadn't moved or said anything since the truck had started. She'd wrapped her arms around my legs and appeared to have no intention of letting go.

"Are you okay?" I asked."What do you think?"

"I don't know."

"What the hell are we doing here, Lou? Who are these people, and where are we going? How do we know these two bozos up front aren't the drug runners that Johnson was talking about? That old man is going to get us killed."

"I know, I know," I said. I let her go on, and she did. It wasmore of what she'd said the night before, and I didn't have anything better to say than I had then.

Her rant ended when we pulled up to what looked like some kind of store. Its one light was inside and consisted of a lightbulb dangling from an electrical cord. One of the men got out and wentin. He said something to the man inside, who gave him a package. He got back into the truck, and we were on the move again.

The dark surrounded us once more. The only light came from the truck's dashboard and the reflection of its headlights off a light fog that had started to develop. The air was getting heavier. We bumped along the dirt road, which appeared to be taking us deeper into the jungle. It was closing in around us.

Jay was silent again, and I thought it best to leave well enough alone. I certainly had no insights into where we were going or what would happen next.

Suddenly, we burst into a clearing. The fog was thick, but through it I could see lights. The truck rumbled across the clearing and cameto a stop next to another truck. The driver and passenger got out and came around to the rear, opened the tailgate, and helped us down. They said something in broken English, but I still didn'tunderstand. They pointed to a light in the fog and ushered ustoward it. We came to a door, which the driver opened and motionedus through. I could hear voices. Johnson's voice. The driver led us through a maze of rooms filled with electronic equipment and opened the door to a large room. Johnson; Thomas; and, I assume, Bert Carson was watching a large computer screen. What they weretalking about, I didn't have the faintest idea. They stopped, and Johnson turned.

"This is Dr. Bert Carson, my colleague and friend. Bert, this is Lou and Jay. We asked them along. We couldn't risk leaving them behind."

Thomas spoke up. "They are my friends, Dr. Carson. They helped me to locate you and Dr. Johnson. I could not have gotten here without them."

Carson nodded. "I see."

It seemed that Johnson had had no difficulty convincing Bert of Thomas's identity. I wondered why that was so easy. In fact, Johnson's reaction to Thomas had been the same. Maybe NASA scientists knew something the rest of us didn't. In fact, I'm positive of that, on many levels.

"I'm sure you folks are hungry and tired," said Bert. "Let's get you some food. Damon will show you to your room and round up what we have in the kitchen. I think you should accompany us tomorrow. It'll be safer than leaving you here."

Safer? I wasn't sure what he meant, but I'd find out soon enough. Damon spoke excellent English. He showed us to our room, whereour bags were waiting.

Jay still hadn't said anything since we'd arrived, so I figured it would be a good time for me to take a shower before we had food. At least I could put off facing her a little longer. She apparently had the same idea. We took turns.

I hadn't really noticed the room when we first came in, justheaded for the bath. But with some time to kill waiting for Jay, I looked around. Fairly basic: a double bed, bureau, an old bamboo dresser with a large mirror. A small closet. A straight-back chair. Two oil table lamps. One electric light, which Damon had turned on when we entered the room.

Jay came out and said that she was ready to go. Damon was atthe door. He showed us to a small dining room on the other side of the hall and left. We sat down and waited. The fare for the evening was two large tamales and a variety of sauces, chips, and two Inca colas. He said we could have cervaza, beer, if we liked, rather than the cola. We both opted for the beer.

Half a bottle through, Jay's mood seemed to brighten. She actuallysmiled. Just as I was about to say something, Johnson came in. He was still bright and bushy-tailed, just as he'd been when we leftCocoa Beach. I was getting a little tired of Mr. Sunshine.

"So, enjoying your meal?" he asked.

We grunted something. I don't remember what.

"Well, it was a long flight, so get some rest, because we'll be up early in the morning. We have another full day ahead of us."

And with that, he started to leave.

"Wait a minute. Where are we going tomorrow? And what did Bertmean about it being safer if we went along?" I asked.

"We're going to be doing a little spelunking—you know, caving, tomorrow."

"I think we'd prefer to stay behind and rest."

"Yes," agreed Jay. "Crawling around a cave doesn't really appeal tome."

"Well, I'm afraid you'll need to come with us. The drug runners willsoon learn that you're here, and a sideline of theirs is kidnappingand extortion. At least they might decide that you could show them where the plane is hidden."

"We couldn't," Jay countered. I nodded in agreement.

"Well, I know that, but they don't. And they might not figure that out until they'd gotten their kicks trying to convince you to talk." "Okay, okay," I said. "We'll go. But why a cave? Won't we be goingin the wrong direction? Thomas's friends are . . . up there," I said, waving my hands in the air.

"Well," said Johnson, "I don't know the whole story yet, but Bert wants to show Thomas a communication device—at least that's what he thinks it is—that some of the locals found in a nearby cave. It appears to have some connection to the work that he's been doingin Bermuda."

"Okay," I said, with some hesitation.

We finished our beers. Damon didn't offer a second. One to a customer, I guess. We went back to our room and got ready for bed.I was the first in.

"So," said Jay, when she climbed in, "do we really know any more than we did?"

"I . . . I don't know," I said.

Communication device? A connection to Bermuda? Why wouldThomas know anything about that? I thought that Johnson wasn't telling us the whole story. He'd whispered to Carson somethingabout us being exposed. But exposed to what? To Thomas, I guess. Maybe he has some sort of illness or disease. Maybe by spending all that time with him in the car, we might have contracted it, I thought.That's pretty far out, but so is everything else.

"Well, I don't trust any of them," said Jay."We wanted a change, didn't we?"

"Speak for yourself, bucko. What I wouldn't give to be putting upstock in Jane's toy store."

"You don't mean that, do you?" I asked.

"Well, it would be a lot safer. We wouldn't be trying to avoid drugrunners and kidnappers."

"You do have a point," I conceded.

Jay rolled over to her side of the bed.

"Well, good night," she said. "I can't wait to see what tomorrow will bring."

I laid there for a while in the dark. I was tired but didn't feel like sleeping. Lynn, my kids, my job seemed a million miles away. Part of another life. For some reason, I started thinking about sex. Maybe because I was in bed with Jay. It's been nonexistent for years with anyone. And speaking of sex, I'm confused about a lot of what's going on in this world about sex. I mean, women's liberation was enough. But now? Half of Lynn's friends are lesbians, and I suspected that the other half were bisexual. Some days I wondered about her.

And gay marriage—now, don't get me wrong, I'm not anti-gay or anything like that. But whatever happened to it being okay to be straight? For a man and a woman to get married? And now we've got this transgender thing, which I don't understand at all. And they just added a "q." For queer, I guess. Someone told me that. I'm sorry, but they lost me on that one. I thought that "queer" was one of those politically incorrect words. I'm just sick of all of this. Well, I should say that to Lynn. I'm just sick of all this. This craziness. But I haven't, and I probably won't. I'd feel guilty for some reason.

And while I'm on this rant, I'd like to know why they call Playboy pornography now. I really don't understand that. Sure, pornography is a bad thing. When I see this new stuff on the Internet, I feel dirty all over. I guess you could say that I hate pornography. But Playboy is pretty mild stuff. Innocent in some ways. Like an old friend. Familiar. I hear they're going to open a new Playboy Club in New York City. Someone told me recently that "retro" is in. Maybe the clubs will make a comeback. Who knows in this world? In many ways, it felt like we've stepped back into the 50s or 60s. A lot of people think that's a good thing. And things were a hell of a lot simpler then, I think. I guess. But was America greater then than now? I don't know. For whom? At least for white men? Trump certainly thinks it was. Maybe he's right. But he's done some pretty crazy things since he's been in office. I don't know anymore. I say that a lot.

CHAPTER 9

It was another early morning. Damon was at the door at six, asking if we were up and ready for breakfast. Breakfast. That was an interesting matter. No bacon and eggs for these guys. How about a tamale? At first, I thought we were having leftovers from supper, and I started to ask for a beer, but Damon explained that this was a breakfast tamale. A staple in Peru and very good. "Mui bien." And he was right. It was good, even if you had to have it with "cafe negro." That's black coffee.

Just as we were finishing, Bert came in to say that we had to leave immediately. I didn't ask why; we were off to the races again. We didn't need to take anything, just ourselves, he said.

Once again, we loaded into the back of the pickup truck. But this time we could see where we were going. We were following another pickup. I managed to stand up long enough to look over the cab and recognized Bert, Thomas in the middle, and Johnson in the cab of the truck in front of ours. I struggled back to a seated position and got ready for another long, bumpy ride, if getting ready for such a thing is possible. And the ride was everything it promised to be. But it wasn't that long. We pulled off the main dirt road onto one thatthe jungle was trying to reclaim, and then we stopped.

Damon climbed out of the cab. "We must walk from here," he said. So, we climbed down and started to walk. As I was starting to catch up with Bert, Thomas, and Johnson, two of Bert's men appeared from the side of the road and hoisted Thomas piggy-back style onto the largest man. Thomas objected at first but finallyrealized that he couldn't make the climb without help. He wrapped his arms around the neck of the man. I was relieved. I knew that he couldn't go very far on foot.

Thank God, it was a short walk. Jay kept complaining and asking meabout poisonous snakes. I assured her that there weren't any, which I'm sure she knew wasn't true. I guess she'd gotten used to me telling her things that weren't true, sometimes to reassure her, but other times justto shut her up. Fortunately, or unfortunately for me, she's a smart woman. I think that she can usually tell the difference. If she thought thatI was just trying to get her to stop talking, she'd tell me so. In addition, an old ankle injury was starting to bother me. After years of physical therapy, I still had it. It just happened one morning. I was going up the stairs to my office and felt my ankle pop. Just a sign of getting old, I guess. I wasn't looking forward to old age. It hadn't been kind to my mother, who suffered for years with rheumatoid arthritis before it finally killed her. Finally, we were there. There, meaning a hole in the side of a mountain. I made my way to the head of the pack. Bert began distributing miners' helmets, each with an electric light, and emergency air-packs, bothof which had been charged at the cabin and brought along. He explained their operation. If a fire erupted, we could use the pack toget back to a safe place, but he didn't really explain where a safe place would be.

"Wait a minute, wait a minute," I said. "Before we risk life and limb in this hole in the ground, I think you guys have a little explaining todo."

"Yes, yes," Johnson said. Bert began nodding in agreement."We will," said Bert.

"I've—I mean, we've—got some questions about all of this." "I'm sure you do, but please get in the man-car." He gestured toward a little metal car with seats in it. I'd seen one as a child in a West Virginia coalmine museum dedicated to the history of coalmining. My family and I were on one of our rare vacations. All of us seemed to be having a good time, which was unusual. Ordinarily, mom and dad would get into it after the first dayor so, and the rest of the trip would consist of skirmishes between them, ending in icy silence or sometimes in a royal knockdown drag out winner take all. My brother and I tried to keep our heads down and stay out of it.

The two men who'd helped Thomas enter the cave were now loading him into the man-car.

"Okay, okay," I said. "But don't start this damn thing up until you tell us where we're going."

"This is a mine, not just a cave," said Bert. "Some locals found a deposit of copper in here a few years ago. It was easy to mine. By our standards, it wouldn't be worth the effort, but by theirs it was. Copper's value has certainly increased."

"Yes," I said impatiently.

"So, one day they broke through a wall of the mine and found themselves in a large room. They immediately noticed a stone structure that looked like it had been made by humans. One of the miners knew that I'm a scientist and thought I might be interested."

The car was starting to move. I didn't object. Bert took a seat in the first car and turned to face us.

"So, I came down. They knew that I was studying magnetic fields in the area around Cusco and Machu Picchu, so they asked me to bring my equipment. They told me that their compasses didn't work in the cave, and when they placed them near the stone structure, they began to spin like crazy.

"So, I brought my instruments down. That was two years ago. I haven't left. It's taken that long to map the magnetic fields. The stone structure, they call it an altar, runs for many miles back into and up the mountain. It appears to run under Cusco and toward Machu Picchu. We haven't gotten that far yet."

"Who built it and why?" Jay asked.

"We don't know. We think it might have been an escape tunnel." The whole time Bert had been talking, Thomas had said nothing. The man-car stopped.

"Here we are," said Bert.

He shone his light on a gaping hole in the tunnel wall. "This is where they broke through." There appeared to be no activity in the mine. The mining equipment was covered in dust and looked like it hadn't been used for some time.

"Is this mine abandoned?" I asked.

"You could say that. After the breakthrough, a number of the men working in the mine became ill, and numerous accidents occurred. The locals started saying that there was bad energy in the mine, especially in the late morning and early afternoon, when the magnetic energy was at its highest. So now no one works in the mine. Even my guys are afraid to come here, except in early morning and late afternoon."

"Where's Thomas?" I asked."Over there," said Jay.

Thomas had climbed out of the man-car and was standing in the middle of the cavernous room, directly in front of the altar. But he was looking up at the ceiling. As I approached him, he pointed up.

"Dr. Johnson," he called. When Johnson arrived at his side, they both peered up.

"Yes," Johnson said. "Yes, I see."Bert joined them. Jay and I couldn't figure out at first what was so interesting. But as my eyes adjusted to the dark, I began to see what they were looking at. It appeared to be a crude drawing of our solar system. Icounted the nine planets I remembered Pluto included. But way outbeyond Pluto was a tenth planet. That was the one at whichThomas was pointing his light. I assumed it was his home. So,what was a drawing of our solar system doing in the cave? Well, I didn't have to wait long to find out. Thomas began to talk.

"Dr. Johnson, Dr. Carson, I have not been completely honest with you. Before the machines took control, my people traveled to your world. They lived among the inhabitants of Peru and were treated as gods until humans from another part of your world came here. My people took refuge with the Inca king in Machu Picchu."

"You mean the Spanish," Johnson said.

"Yes," said Thomas. "The Spanish brought with them a horrible plague to which my people had no resistance. Our historians tell us that the plague apparently killed all our people, as no one returned from this world."

"Well," said Bert, breaking into the conversation, "by chance, we'vefound a structure similar to this on a small island in Hamilton

Bay in Bermuda." "Yes," said Thomas. "That is consistent with the history of the colony as told by our people. This is a very old transporter."

"Like on Star Trek?" asked Jay. "Well, no," said Johnson.

"Actually, it is similar," said Thomas. "This device allowed our people to travel across your planet without being detected."

"But what's most interesting about the stone altar in Bermuda is where it leads," said Bert. "It runs into the sea, across the Barrier Reefs that surround Bermuda, and into the deepest part of the ocean. We've taken magnetic readings down as far as our equipmentwill go, but we have no idea where the structure terminates."

"I do not know," said Thomas. "According to our historians, thelast transmission from the few colonists who had survived the plaguesaid that they were abandoning this site."

I lost track of what they were saying. A strange feeling had come over me. Maybe it was the bad air Bert had talked about. My eyes were watering. I felt like I was going to cry, but not because I was sad. Because I was grateful to be a part of all this. A being from another world and a space scientist wanted my help. The Peruvian jungle, and me in the middle of all of it. When I tuned back in, Thomas was saying that the New Horizons space probe launched by NASA a few years ago had completed a fly-by of Pluto and was now entering deep space and might encounter his home planet. "The machines will see this as an aggressive act bythe people of Earth. New Horizons should be diverted or destroyed by NASA."

Johnson and Carson were arguing this point. They'd been involved in the development of New Horizons and were proud of the accomplishment.

Carson spoke first. "Thomas, it'll be years before the probe enters your planet's orbit. And even then, it will probably miss it completely."

"That's assuming it's still operating and sending signals back tous," said Johnson. "I think it's unlikely that the machines will even detect its presence."

Raymond, who'd been quiet, entered the conversation with some passion. "That's ridiculous! Are we men or mice? We can't allow these oversized laptops to control us."

"The machines will destroy us and your world if you   resist," warned Thomas. "Your technology is not, I think, capable of resisting their control." Johnson and Carson were listening intently to Thomas. Raymond was listening but still shaking his head.

It seemed that living in peace meant allowing our lives to be controlled by a bunch of supercomputers. Granted, as years had passed, we'd given more and more over to our machines. But in our world, they still worked for us. We were still in control. In Thomas's world, they were calling the shots. Now, don't get me wrong. I'm not one of those anti-tech people. It has certainly moved our livesforward. But we're in control. Still, a niggling thought arose in my mind: Maybe we only think we are.

And, of course, the human track record on living together in peace hasn't been too great. Maybe we aren't smart enough to figure that oneout. Perhaps the machines are. The voices of Raymond, Thomas, Johnson, and Carson were getting louder, so I decided to tune in again.I looked at Jay. She seemed confused by all this talk. She moved closerand whispered, "What are they going to do now?"

"I don't know," I said. "I have no idea."

"Well, I guess we can't do anything else but wait, but this place does give me the creeps."

I nodded. "I'm beginning to feel more than the creeps. Johnson seems right about this place." He had told us that spending time in the mine could affectus emotionally. But not necessarily in a bad way. He said that the effect was strongest when the magnetic force was at its peak. And—well, I wasn't really clear about this—but it sometimes made people feel more peaceful and grateful.

"I think we're going to need more than we have to convince nations and corporations to peacefully welcome your people to our world," said Bert. "As you know, fear and suspicion of our neighbors is at an all-time high. There's little cooperation or mutual respectamong the nations and the mega-corporations. It's likely that they'djust compete with each other to take control of the mothership and your people just to have access to the technology and knowledge they believe you bring."

"They would be mistaken," said Thomas. "As I have explained, what you call the 'software' that controls these devices will be destroyed when the mothership touches down. My people no longer have the knowledge or the skill to replicate any of it."

"If the colonists escaped the plague and are still alive, they'd have technology that would be of interest to world authorities," said Johnson. "Yes," said Thomas. "They had the most advanced technology thatour society had at that time. Some of our brightest and mosttalented engineers and scientists were members of the colony."

"If that's true, why didn't they return to your world?" asked Johnson.

"I do not know," said Thomas.

"Perhaps they knew what was coming. The Singularity. The day ofthe machines" offered Raymond.

"It is unclear in our history," said Thomas.

"If they're alive and living at the bottom of the ocean, they would have developed . . . it would be unbelievable what they could have developed," said Johnson.

"We've got to go there and try to communicate with them," said Bert. "They may have developed the technology required to convince our authorities to resist the machines."

"Hey, guys," I interjected, "if these folks haven't been heard from for hundreds of years, maybe they don't want our 'world authorities', or the machines, to know that they're still alive."

"Yes," said Jay. "What if the lost colony doesn't want to be found?""That is possible," said Thomas. "But time is short. Our mothership will soon be in range of your observatories and radio telescopes. The machines tracking our journey will know that we have arrived.""Well, I don't think we have any choice," said Bert.

"I agree," said Johnson.

"The issue is, how will we get the device in Hamilton Bay to work? We've had no success up to this point," said Bert.

Thomas continued to look carefully at the stone altar. "I think that the communication device I am carrying is based on this transporter," he said. "But there have been many, many advances since this stone version was created."

Suddenly, one of the two men who had stayed with the trucks appeared from the mine shaft. After a short conversation in Spanish with Bert, Bert said, "We've got to get back to the camp right now. George will drive you." He looked worried.

"Okay," I said as Bert turned and hurried off in the direction of his truck. I didn't know what was happening, but I knew from the way Bert was acting that something was up, and it wasn't good.

I gave Jay my "I don't know what's coming next" look, and she shrugged and nodded. Bert didn't spare the horses getting back to camp. And I'd thoughtthat the ride in was rough!

When we got back, the place looked abandoned, and it was. No vehicles. No people. Finally, Johnson decided to let Jay and me in on what was going on.

"Ricardo, one of the local drug lords, will be paying us a visit very soon, so we need to get the hell out of Dodge as quickly as is humanly possible. Bert and Raymond will get the plane fueled and ready to fly. Get your stuff together. Damon will drive us to the airstrip."

We did as we were told. After another rough and tumble ride, we arrived at the airstrip.

It was late afternoon. "Are we going to wait till nightfall to fly out of here?" I asked.

"No. Bert tells me that we can't wait," said Johnson.

We'd started to board the plane when a giant SUV—it must have been a Yukon—and two pickups rolled onto the end of the airstrip.

"Ricardo," said Jay.

"I hope Bert can talk his way out of this one," I said.

The vehicles came to a stop in front of the plane. Bert was all smiles. He rushed to shake hands with the man who appeared to be in charge, Ricardo I assumed, and began to show him the plane.Our guest entered the cabin first, followed by Bert and one of Ricardo's "associates."

Ricardo was a small man with large sunglasses that hid his eyes. Clean-shaven, well dressed—overdressed, it appeared to me, given where the hell we were.

"I am Ricardo Deago, a good friend of Dr. Carson's."His English was good. I smiled and nodded.

"I'm Louis Black, and this is Jay Simms. Good to meet you." Ournervousness showed. I fumbled for words, and so did Jay. I wasn'tquite sure what to say to a drug dealer, as I'd never met one before.Thomas had pulled up his hoodie and was pretending to be asleep. Fortunately, Ricardo focused on Jay and ignored Thomas and me. "And you, my lady, I trust that you are enjoying the hospitality of our Dr. Carson?"

Jay nodded. "Yes. Yes. It's a beautiful place . . . Peru."

Bert and Raymond continued to show him and his bodyguards the plane, moving up the aisle toward the cockpit. I noticed that Thomas suddenly had his little black box out. I hoped that he was pointing the thing in the direction of Ricardo and friends. Ricardo was complimentary regarding the plane. Bert and Raymond smiled. And then Ricardo said, "I would very much like to own a fine plane like this. It would be a real asset for my business."

"Well now, it is a fine plane," said Bert, "but it's an experimental model still in development." He looked at Raymond.

"Yes, we're still working the bugs out," Raymond added.

Ricardo looked displeased. "You could stay and work out these 'bugs' for us, no?"

Raymond began to explain that he had commitments at homeand that the instruments and equipment he required were not easily available in the jungle.

The more Raymond tried to explain, the more upset Ricardo became. And then the conversation made a U-turn. But not because of Bert or Raymond. It was Ricardo. His mood and behavior changed visibly. He suddenly began to smile.

"I will respect your wishes, Dr. Carson. I am disappointed that the plane is not yet ready for sale, as it is a such a fine craft, but perhaps we can talk again when these 'bugs ' are managed."

Bert looked surprised by the sudden reversal. I assumed that a man like Ricardo seldom respected anyone or anything and almost never took no for an answer. Bert stopped talking. Then I noticed that Thomas was smiling. He didn't do that much, so it got my attention.

I whispered to him, "Did you do something? To change Ricardo?" He smiled again. "It worked," he said.

Bert was ushering Ricardo and his associate off the plane. Ricardo wasn't objecting. He continued to praise Bert for his kindness and generosity and offered to make a large financial donation to the research that Bert was doing at the mine.

Bert brought up the stairway. He was shaking his head and smiling. Raymond was at the controls with Johnson. The engines roared to life. The plane began to lumber down the airstrip through the tall grass that covered it.

"Well, he did it," I said to Jay.

"That Bert is a smooth one, isn't he?""No, no," I said. "Thomas."

"Thomas? What did he do?"

"I don't know . . . something. I guess Mr. Peace and Love savedthe day, or at least his little black box did. Didn't you see that?"

"No, I'm sorry I didn't. I was busy trying not to wet my pants." Shelaughed.

"Oh." I joined her in laughing. I enjoyed her laughter. The takeoff was smooth. We gained altitude quickly.

"So, Thomas, what did you do? And give me an explanation I can understand."

"I do not know myself the science behind what I did. I did noteven know that it would work until it did. It appeared to me that we needed to take some action quickly or we would lose possession of this vessel. As for an explanation of how it works, it affects brain chemistry, but only temporarily. Mr. Ricardo will be himself in a few hours and even more the sociopath that Dr. Carson described to me earlier today."

"I believe that the transporter in the mine produced the unfamiliar, you might say alien, feelings that affected the workers, similar to those that my device just created in Mr. Ricardo."

"Feelings of gratitude?"

"Yes. I believe you could label them as such."

"I was beginning to feel strange like that just before we left themine," I said.

"You human beings are quite different from us. You considerfeelings of gratitude as strange. To my people, they as normal."

That stopped me. Thomas was right. We are a strange lot. Weinfrequently take the time to appreciate and be grateful for whatever we have in our lives. I thought about Lynn and my kids. I wondered if Lynn had told the girls what was happening. "You dad has run off to Florida with another woman."

Now, that's a really great way to appreciate the ones you love. I needed to rethink this whole thing. Take stock of what I had before I flushed it all. Maybe it was already too late. Just as I was kicking into high gear with another bout of self-doubt and recrimination, Johnson decided to pay the three of us a visit.

"Either of you been to Bermuda before?" he asked Jay and me. "Sure," I said. I'd gone many years ago with Lynn for two weeks one winter. We'd done it as sort of the honeymoon we couldn'tafford when we'd gotten married. We rented an apartment in a house on Hamilton Bay. Beautiful view of Hamilton.

"How about you, Jay?"

"No. Too rich for my blood," she said.

"Well, either one of you got a passport on you?"

Jay said that she'd never had one, and I said that I hadn'tbothered to renew mine. Didn't have any need to. Lynn and I hadn't been out of the country since we went to Bermuda.

"Well, you know, Doc, we weren't planning on leaving the states when we started this trip." "It's okay. We'd never get Thomas through customs anyway. We'regoing to take it slow. We'll arrive in the wee hours of the morning."

"I'm sure you're right about Thomas," I said.

"Bert has a friend in customs, but I'm afraid we're going to have to'crate' the three of you." He made quotation marks in the air and laughed.

"Wait a minute . . ." I began.

"What are you talking about?" Interrupted Jay.

"See these three crates?" Johnson pointed to three wooden crates just behind our chairs. "Luckily they're empty. It may be a little tight, but we'll get you off and onto the truck that's meeting us as quickly as we can."

Thomas nodded. He looked tired. Jay just rolled her eyes and looked scared. She was getting good at that.

"Just enjoy the flight. Bert and I will help you into the crates just before we land. Relax, we did this a few years ago with a couple of graduate students who'd forgotten their passports.

"How'd you get them out of Bermuda when it was time to go home?"

"Bert's friend took care of that. You know, these folks in Bermuda aren't as crazy as the US is now. You might get shot in the US doing this, but here, it's a fine at worst.""Okay," I said.

Doing something significant? Being someone? Well, it certainly had its downside. Good thing that Jay and I weren't claustrophobic—at least, I assumed she wasn't. Thomas, I wasn't sure about.

CHAPTER 10

It was well after midnight when we began our descent. Johnson motioned us toward the shipping crates.

"Okay," he said, "who wants to be first? You can have your choice.""Very funny," I retorted. "They look all the same to me."

"They are," he said. "A crate's a crate."

"Why don't you go first, Lou?" said Jay.

"All right," I agreed with considerable hesitation. I'd never been ina space that small.

"Come on, Lou. We don't have all day to do this," said Johnson.I stepped into the one nearest me and sat down.

"Johnson reached for the lid. He must have seen the expression on my face.

"Okay," he said. "I wasn't planning on nailing the lid on until we'reon the ground." "Thanks." I knew that it might take a little time to adjust to being treated like freight.

Thomas and Jay seemed to take it better than I did. They didn't complain. In fact, they didn't say anything.

Before Johnson nailed the lid down, he gave us a little lesson on being freight.

"Stretch out and brace your feet and arms against the walls of the crate. And be quiet. Try not to move around. Again, brace yourself with your arms and your legs. The crates are marked 'fragile,' and I'll supervise the unloading. The truck should be waiting. Bert knows the customs officer, so it should go smoothly. We're going to an old Navy bunker, not far from the airport. The road is a bit curvy, since it runs by the ocean so—well, you might get a little 'seasick.' Bert says it's not a long ride."

Johnson was right about one thing: The sickness. It was good he gave us barf bags from the plane. Throwing up, or trying not to throw up, kept me busy for most of the ride. I did notice when the truck slowed and pulled into the bunker, though. I heard someone climb onto the back of the truck and begin pulling the lids off of Jay's and Thomas' crates.

"Any time," I said from inside mine. "Hold your horses," Johnson said. "First on, last off. That's how it iswhen you're freight."

When they finally knocked the lid off, the light stung my eyes. We were in a large underground warehouse. Part of a U.S. Navy base that Johnson said had been abandoned in the sixties. He helped me out of the crate.

"Rough ride?" he asked. "How're you feeling now?""Rough," I replied.

"Well, you'll feel better when you get some food in you.""I'm not so sure about that. How are Jay and Thomas?""Just fine," said Johnson.

"Just fine," I echoed and shook my head.

We climbed off the truck, and I followed Johnson through a doorway that led into a long tunnel to the old base cafeteria. Bert was there with Raymond, Jay, Thomas, and a couple of guys I hadn't seen before.

"It's not much," said Bert, "but it's home. Luckily, the freezer and gas stove still work."

I didn't take Johnson up on his offer of food. All I wanted was a hot shower and a comfortable bed. I got the first, but the bed was nothing to write home about. Jay was offered a room of her own, and she took it. I guess we both needed a little alone time.

I had a hard time getting to sleep. I thought about Lynn and my girls. Guilt and gratitude were still having their way with me. And I think Jay sensed that something was different with me. She was always better at that than I was. I was more distant. But I needed tobe.

I wasn't sure anymore, and I was certain she would see that if we talked. So, I hadn't talked much.

When morning came, I tried to sleep in, but Johnson was at my door being Mr. Sunshine. My stomach had settled in the night, and I was hungry. Even though I didn't want to face Jay, I found my way down to the cafeteria.

The boys were having a meeting. Bert, Johnson, Thomas, and two of Bert's associates. Jay was sitting by herself with a cup of coffee. I assumed that she'd finished breakfast.

They fried up a couple of eggs for me and some bacon, even though I wasn't supposed to have it. What the hell. If the boys weren't successful with what they were plotting, the world mightend anyway. A pound or two and a little extra cholesterol wouldn't make much difference. As I was waiting for my breakfast, I noticed that the cook looked familiar. He kept staring at me, so I finally asked, "Do we know eachother?"

He turned to face me and, before he could speak, I said, "Kenny." "Yes. Yes, Mr. Black, it's me."

"What are you doing here?" I didn't really know Kenny or his family. He'd worked in a Greek restaurant that Jay and I used to go to for those lunches we had.

"So, my Uncle Bert decided that I should visit and travel with him. He said it's what my mom wanted. So, I said sure. I get to travel a lot with Uncle Bert. He put me to work here. He's a great guy."

It's a small world, I thought. I didn't know that Carson had any connections to Maine, much less to Kenny.

"I'll be going out with you guys. He wants me to work the galley."

"Great," I said. "I'll see you later." It was news to me that we were going out. But Jay and I were still the last to know anything. I guesseveryone still thought that we were just along for the ride.

He handed me my breakfast and smiled again. Jay was looking in my direction, so I joined her.

"How are you, honey?" I said, trying to sound cheerful."Fine, I guess," she responded. "And you?" "Oh, I'm okay," I avoided her eyes.

"No, you aren't," she said. "So how do you really feel?"

"I don't know." I tried to stall. "All of this business with Thomasand Johnson has got me a little confused."

"Lou, I don't think that's all that's confusing you."

"You're right," I kept staring at the table. "I guess I'm havingsecond thoughts."

"Well, you should," she said. "You haven't really involved me muchin your little fantasy about running off to Florida."

"Well, I thought I had," I said. "I would have, if I'd gotten thechance."

"Lou, joking with me about going to Florida with you isn't reallyinvolving me in the plan."

"Well, I thought . . ."

"And meeting me after work with your car packed and a full tankof gas doesn't exactly give me much time to make a decision."

Of course, she was right. "Well, I guess..."

"You're right. It would have to be a guess because you neverreally asked me how I felt."

"I'm not sure you would have told me."

"Oh, Lou," she said, looking exasperated. "You're right, Jay. I'm sorry. I love you," I added.

"I know you do, and I love you, but I don't know that this decisionis about love. It's about doing what's right for all of us."

"Yes, yes," I agreed.

"And not just what's right for you. Your wife is a good person. Godknows she's put up with you for all these years. She deserves betterthan what you're giving her right now."

I nodded.

"And your kids. How are they going to feel about this? You want grandchildren, don't you?"

She didn't wait for me to answer.

"I know you do. And you want them to be a part of your life. And me, do you know what I want? I don't know that I want to deal withan ex-wife or children or grandchildren of yours that might resentme for breaking up their 'happy home.'"

"But . . ." I began but then stopped, and we just sat there.Not for long, though. Johnson came over to our table.

"Did you kids have a good breakfast?"We nodded and mumbled something.

"You're going to have to spend the day with us. Bert and Thomasaren't comfortable leaving you here alone. They aren't sure that you'd be here when we got back."

I was beginning to feel a bit irritated with everything, especiallyMr. Sunshine. "Where would we go, and how would we get off this island without a passport or our help? I'm sure we're not going anyplace until you guys finish this goose chase you're on." I sounded disgusted and meant to.

"Well, you're right about that. But I think that you've missed the fact that we're all part of something much bigger than a goose chase. Don't you understand what we're dealing with?"

Perhaps I didn't or just wasn't in the mood to understand. This morning was one of those times when my emotions had taken control of my thinking.

"Where to?" I asked.

"A small island on the edge of Hamilton Bay. Be ready in a half-hour."

I started to get up and head back to my room to pack for the "cruise," like the good doctor instructed, but Jay grabbed my hand. I think she realized that I was pretty upset.

"Lou, don't look so sad. You and I have a connection. Something that we don't share with anyone else. I think we'll always have that, no matter what happens."

I smiled. "Yes, you're right," I said. "I'm sure you're right." I lookedaway.

I think I realized for the first time what she was saying. What she'd said many times before. As Bogart would say to Bergman, "We'll always have Paris." But was that it? Was that all there was? Allthere would be? I felt angry with myself. God knows that wasa familiar feeling. At Jay? No. Well . . . yes. At Lynn? I wasn't sure.I didn't know who or what I was angry at. Thomas?Johnson? Everyone and everything.

Yes, I was feeling just a little angry and cynical, as I threw—and the word is "threw"—my stuff together. I didn't liked cruises that much, not that I'd been on many. Well, to be truthful, only one. I got seasick. Spent most of the time in our cabin. Lynn was a saint. She took care of my sorry ass. I think she did have some fun with the other couple we'd booked with. They were nice. A girlfriend of Lynn'sfrom work and her husband. Lynn was great at setting these things up. They always reminded me of blind dates and often worked out the same way. Not good. But Lynn meant well. She said we— meaning me—needed more friends. I usually went along with a dinner out or having a couple over for dessert. But I would have to say, my heart really wasn't in it, and I guess it showed. I know it showed. Maybe I should have taken it more seriously and tried harder. In the last few years, Lynn seemed to stop trying. Why should she if I wasn't going to? Well, as they say, hindsight is 20/20,and I seemed to be having a lot of that lately.

I suppose by now you're wondering how I got involved with Jay a second time. When I told you that we were young and foolish, we still were when our paths crossed again. I'd been working with the firm I just left, Hayes, Edwards & Peabody, for just a few years. Jay was a new hire as an administrative assistant, and we were assignedto work on the same audit team.

Well, we ended up working, shall we say, very closely. Like old times. I'm not proud of the affair. I don't even know exactly how it happened, but it did. I don't think I'd let something like that happen again at my work.

I'd been married for a few years. Deborah was just a year old, and Lynn was pregnant with Marie. As I said, I'm not proud of what happened. Oh, I can give the usual excuses. We weren't "communicating." All we ever talked about was the baby and her pregnancy.

But I did wrong.

The affair went on for quite a while. I tried to break it off. Jayagreed that it was wrong. You can't go back in time. We finally didend it. I don't think that Lynn ever found out. We were very careful.My OCD has its advantages. And I certainly never told her about Jay.I've wondered over the years why—why I got involved with Jay again and felt so strongly about her. There are the obvious reasons. The communication thing I just mentioned, and the fact that Jay was—and still is—a beautiful and sexy woman.

But there was more to it than that. I've thought about it a lot. Jay and I come from the same place. We understand each other. Jay grew up without a dad. He died when she was only eight ornine. And I might as well have grown up without one. I think my family would have been better off if he'd died. He drank like a fish. As my dad would say, he lived his life "balls out." I think that my mother hated that expression about as much as she hated him. If you haven't heard it before, it means to take risks. I think he took a lot of them in Vietnam to win all those medals he never talkedabout. But I don't know if that's true. I never got to know my dad. Even when he was around, he wasn't really there. My mom finally had enough and divorced him. He's dead now. Got run over by a caron the strip in

Las Vegas. My brother, who's eight years older, told me that dad was drunk and wandered out in front of it.

Like Jay's mom, mine ended up having to work two jobs to support the family. She didn't have much time for me or my brother. Also like Jay, I was the youngest. She had an older sister who really didn't like having to take care of Jay. She hasn't seen much of her sister since her mom's death. That was quite a few years ago. The same for my brother. I haven't seen him since our mom's funeral.

I guess Jay and I sort of raised ourselves. But I wonder sometimes if either one of us has really grown up completely. I think we both still miss what we didn't have. Our lousy childhoods sort of stunted our growth as people. Like they used to say about smoking at an early age.

Now, Lynn, on the other hand, came from what I'd call a "normal family," if there is such a thing. Her dad is gone. Died in his sixties. She and her mom and sisters are close. Call each other all the time. I didn't know her dad very well, but I think he was a good man. A good provider for his wife and his children. I've been that, up till now. So, you can see that Jay and I have a lot in common. We really do know what the other is thinking before they say it. We understand each other. It's funny how those early years with our parents have had such an effect on us and continue to affect us, even at this point in our lives.

CHAPTER 11

Jay and I met the boys in the dining room. Kenny had made us all lunches. Johnson was finishing his last cup of coffee. He could pound 'em down like liquor. He said he'd developed an addiction to coffee when he'd gotten involved with AA and sobered up. That was quite a few years ago, before he lapsed back into his real addiction. I don't know what he'd say he was doing now, but I don't think he'd had a drink since we left the states.

We boarded a small boat that resembled one of the ferries we'd taken when Lynn and I'd had that short vacation. I really don't know much about boats or the ocean. I just know that the water was calmand the air warm. Bert said that the water in the harbor usually was.We were inside the reef that surrounded and protected Bermuda. Outside the reef, the sea was always rougher.

Jay and I stood for a while on the upper deck. The sun on my face felt good. It reminded me of the few times when Mom, my brother, and I had gone to the beach. We didn't go often, even though we lived near the ocean. Mom said that it made her nervous. Theocean. I never understood that. I don't think that my brother did, either. But at least we had a big backyard. I remember lying downon the warm grass in summer and spreading my arms and legs like Iwas making a snow angel. God, the warmth felt so good. Andlooking up at the blue sky and the clouds. I wished that I could just float off with one of them to another world. A better one than this. One with parents who loved each other and their kids, with fathers who came home after work sober, and mothers who weren't afraidof their own shadows.

We could see Hamilton in the distance. Bert pointed out the smallisland that was our destination. It was coming up fast. We'd been onthe water for less than a half-hour, and Jay was being awfully quiet..

We made land and went ashore, as they used to say in the old pirate movies I loved as a kid. They were a great distraction. I would dream of sailing off to foreign lands. I'd be the captain, and my ship would be the biggest and best pirate ship on the high seas. The

Blackhawk. I used to spend hours drawing pictures of it. It's cannons and deck guns. I'd plot the course. And no one would dare to challenge me and the Blackhawk. Well, this ship certainly wasn't the Blackhawk, and I wasn't the captain plotting the course. We followed Bert up a path that took us toward the center of the island. The highest point, Bert said. But stilljust a few feet above sea level. We came to a clearing carved out of the thick vegetation. In it stood an ugly building with metal walls, a windowless roof, and a metal door.

"Ah, here we are," said Bert. "Not many people even know this exists."

And why should they know or care? I thought.

Bert pulled a set of keys from his pocket. Johnson, Thomas, and Raymond lined up with anticipation. Jay and I just trailed along. That seemed to be our role.

Bert opened the door and flipped a switch. A generator on the other side of the building came to life, and the lights inside flickered on. In the center of the building was a stone formation like the one we'd seen in the mine near Machu Picchu.

"We traced it here," said Bert. "This was buried for centuries. Apparently, the English never found it, or if they did, they ignored it. Maybe they thought it was a natural rock formation or the handiworkof some castaways with stone chisels and time on their hands. "Unfortunately, a Chinese research team has taken an interest in what we've been doing out here. They apparently tried to break intothe building a few days ago. The alarm sounded, but they took off before security showed up. I have my doubts about their archeological interest in the island, which is what they'd told my customs friend when they entered the country a few weeks ago. I think they're working for the Chinese government and are really interested in the magnetic field and where it leads."

The boys were now standing in a circle around the stone altar. Jay and I stepped in close enough that we could hear what they were saying.

"The problem is," said Bert, "we don't know how to activate it. Thesignal we followed here is very weak. We assume that the altaracted as a transformer does for electricity, boosting the power of thesignal. Can you help us with that, Thomas?"

Thomas didn't speak as he walked slowly around the altar. Thenhe stopped in front of it.

"Before the machines took control of our ancient texts, I readsome that contained information about the colony. You are correct. The structure did serve to strengthen the signal. This appears to be one of the solar ones. Help me to get up there, please," said Thomas, pointing to the top of the altar.

"Well, now be careful," said Johnson. "You're not that steady on your feet."

Bert pulled a ladder over and Thomas began climbing.

"I'll give you a boost," said Johnson, as he climbed on behind Thomas.

"As you prefer," said Thomas. "Yes, I am correct. The solar cells are here, near the top of the altar. They are just corroded so badly that they may not respond to sunlight."

"Well," said Bert, "there's only one way to find out. Let's clean them up."

"Yes," said Thomas. "And you must open the roof."

Thomas looked at his little black box. "The top of the altar should be in direct alignment with the sun at one P.M., Atlantic time. That is three hours from now. The sun should be directly overhead."

So, we waited. Bert and his men climbed onto the roof. He said he'd thought that they might need to open it to the sky, so they'd installed the metal panels to slide back easily.

Everything was going along quite peachy until we heard a boat approaching the island. "We've got company," said Johnson.

"Who?" I asked.

Before he could answer, Bert was ordering his guys, Kenny included, to form a welcoming party for our company. "There are only three of them," he said.

"Who?" I asked again.

"The damn Chinese. Research, my foot," said Johnson.

"They're here to check on what we are doing. But this time,they're going to get a big surprise," said Bert.

"You're not going to hurt them... or kill them?" asked Jay, looking and sounding alarmed.

"What? No, of course not," said Bert, looking surprised at herquestion. "But they're going to be our guests for a while."

The next thing I knew, Bert's guys were herding three young meninto the clearing. They looked Chinese to me, but what do I know?

"What are you doing? This is against the law! Let us go!" They putup quite a fuss.

"We will," said Bert, "but not right now. Tie them up and blindfoldthem. Over there, away from the building."

The three continued to complain. Bert told his guys to gag them,and they did. "Don't worry. I'm sure your friends will be looking for you, though hopefully not for a few hours."

One o'clock was approaching. The sun was high. We stood aroundthe altar, waiting to see what magic would happen when the sun's light struck the solar cells that had been thoroughly cleaned by Johnson and Bert.

Thomas stood in front of the altar. He looked like he was deep in thought. The light began to strike the solar cells. At first, they sparkled in the early afternoon light like dark crystals. Then they began to glow, a faint and then brighter dark red that rapidlychanged to dark blue.

Thomas hadn't changed his posture in front of the altar. He placed his hands on two "pads"—I guess that's what they were. There wasa humming sound from inside the altar. No one, not even Johnson, said anything. We had our eyes locked on Thomas and the "structure." Thomas placed his black box between his hands. The humming changed into a series of musical notes that Thomas's blackbox repeated. I mean, it was like Close Encounters of the Third Kind.These two machines were talking to each other through music. The connection between them became faster and more intense. Jay andI stepped back. She covered her ears. Finally, it stopped. The humming returned and then died away. The glow of the solar panels returned to dark red and then the altar fell silent.

"I have it," said Thomas. "We must go. They are waiting for us."

Johnson, Raymond and Bert looked excited and elated. Jay and Ididn't.

"Who's waiting for us?" I asked.

"They are," Bert said. "I told you they were here.""But where?" I asked.

"Out there." He waved his hand toward the open ocean. "Thomashas the coordinates."

"We're going out there?""Yes, outside the reef."

"Isn't that dangerous? Isn't that one of the deepest parts of the ocean?"

"Yes, yes!" said Johnson. "Aren't you excited?" He was obviously ecstatic.

"Well, yes, I guess I am," I said. "I don't need to tell you againthat I get seasick. Is that okay?" I sounded stupid. Once again, we were along for the ride.

"Relax. I've got some Dramamine with me," said Johnson. As we were preparing to leave, I noticed Bert's men putting what looked to me like explosives around the altar.

"What's that for?" I asked Johnson.

"That's so our visitors and their friends don't follow us."

"You're going to blow this thing up?"

"Yes. With all the construction happening on the islands in the bay,no one will probably even notice the sound. Besides, it will give the Chinese 'archaeologists' something to try to put back together."

So, we were off again, but only God, and Thomas, knew where. When we were a few hundred yards out from the dock, Bert set off the charge. Johnson was right. The sound of the explosion was muffled by the woods surrounding the structure. A puff of blue-gray smoke appeared above the island but quickly dissolved in the breezeblowing in from the reef.

We headed out from the island and Bermuda. At first, the sea was calm. As we crossed the reef and approached the open ocean, though, the wind picked up and the water became rougher. I tried very hard to not become seasick this time. Johnson's Dramamine was taking its time kicking in. I focused on the horizon, like they say to do, but it didn't help that much.

"You okay?" asked Jay.

"Sure, sure," I said. From the color of my complexion, I'm sure sheknew I was lying.

The sky began to change, too. On the horizon was a large formation of dark clouds, like before a snowstorm. Storm clouds. The weather had never interested me much, except when it was really bad. The heat I could take, but not the cold and snow. Especially the ice. I liked it when I was a kid. My brother and I used to make snowmen in our backyard and sneak off to a pond down theroad from our house that would usually be frozen over by January. We didn't have ice skates. Mom couldn't afford them. And I doubt that she would have bought them for us if she'd had the money. Shealways worried about us getting hurt, drowning, getting run over by a car. You name it. But we had a good time running and sliding around on the ice. I don't think she ever found out about the pond. We'd sneak off after she took her medication and would be out of it for the next few hours.

Of course, all things change when we grow up. At least it did for me. I'm no longer a fan of ice and snow. Lynn and I did take the girls skating. Well, she did most of that. I never learned to skate. I didn't think I had the time. And I was afraid of breaking an ankle and missing work. Things were tight enough without losing time and pay.

Needless to say, we were in Bermuda, so I doubted that it was going to snow. But what would happen next, I didn't know.

Johnson came over, I guess to check on me. I thought that talking to him might take my mind off my churning stomach and my dizzy head.

"Are we following the signal?" I asked.

"Yes," said Johnson. "It's getting stronger. It shouldn't be too longnow."

"Till what?" I asked.

"Contact." He was pacing about. He could hardly contain himself. I assumed that meant contact with Thomas's clan. The last colonyfolks.

"How?" I asked.

"I don't know," said Johnson. "They'll decide."

Our ship was heading into a fog bank. As we proceeded, the fog became thicker. Soon it was difficult to see the person standing nextto you. This was not doing my seasickness any good. To say the least, the fog was disorienting. I started to think that the ship was starting to spin around slowly. But that wasn't possible,I was sure. It was just my stomach and my crazy head.

"Lou, do you feel that?" asked Jay.

"What?" I asked.

"The ship. It feels like it's beginning to . . . spin."

"Can't be," I said. "Can't be."

"Well, I think it is," said Jay.

"No. Not the boat. It's . . . it's the water that's spinning. We're justmoving with it, I think. Where's Johnson? Let's ask him."

But we'd lost track of him in the fog.

"I bet he's on the bridge or wheelhouse or whatever you call the place they steer this thing from," I said.

"Are we being pulled down? asked Jay. "I feel like we're descending. But that isn't possible. Is it?" She again looked and sounded alarmed.

The fog began to clear. We could see a patch of blue sky above us. But all around us was a wall of water. We were descending, being sucked down. The sea was spinning around us. We were in the center of a giant vortex— like water being funneled down a giant drain. The patch of sky grew smaller. The sea continued to spin around us. Jay and I hugged each other and closed our eyes. God onlyknew what was going to happen next. We certainly didn't.

Strange sounds started coming from below the ship. We looked over the side. The water continued to part. Just like in that movie with Charlton Heston playing Moses.

The sounds grew louder. They're hard to describe. Like an air compressor on steroids.

Below us, the sea bubbled like a witch's cauldron. The noisebecame louder as the boat settled into the brew. We were floating again. Our slide into the depths of the sea slowed. Above us, we heard a large metal gate closing—at least, I guess that's what it was.The blue patch of sky disappeared as the sea began to close above us, and the walls of water started to sink into the boiling brew belowus. A strange blue light filled the large room with metal sides thatthe ship now floated in.

The compressor sound began to fade as if someone somewhere had turned a switch off. The bubbling ceased. The sea was calm again.

CHAPTER 12

We waited, saying nothing. A door opened to our left and a metal bridge was extended to the ship.

"We have been waiting for you," a voice said. "Please join us."

Johnson and the boys were all smiles. Jay and I weren't. They couldn't wait to meet our hosts and whispered excitedly to each other as they piled onto the metal bridge. Thomas led the way. As usual, Jay and I brought up the rear. This had all the earmarks of a bad remake of **Twenty Thousand Leagues under the Sea.**

We entered a large room. Bright and, yes, "sunny," if you can believe that. Sunny to the point that it actually hurt my eyes. I looked over at Thomas. Fortunately, he already had on his sunglasses. As we got used to the light, we could see four figures standing at the end of the room, dressed in what looked to me like decontamination suits. "Yes," said the voice. "Please forgive any inconvenience, but we must insist on scanning and decontaminating anyone entering our world from the Earth's surface."

I thought these guys are reading our thoughts.

"Yes," said Thomas. But before he could say more, the voice spokeagain.

"You are aware of our history, that terrible diseases centuries ago nearly destroyed our colony."

As he spoke, one of the four figures examined each of us.

Apparently, we were okay, because a wall in the large room opened. Three creatures were standing there. Short little guys. I swear, they looked just like E.T. Much shorter than Thomas but the same big eyes, no hair, and light gray skin, dressed in what looked like white hospital gowns. Honest.

The voice continued. "We left Peru centuries ago to escape human diseases. We chose Bermuda because it was uninhabited and far from your people. But it was not long until they came. Fortunately, our scientists had been planning for such a time. It has taken us many centuries, but we have created what you will see."

I swear this guy wasn't moving his lips. No one was. I began to wonder, was the voice in the room or in my head? "He must be telepathic," I whispered to Jay.

"Yes, we are," the voice said. "We communicate with thought."

"And you can apparently read minds," I said.

"Yes, we can, if we so choose. I am sure that you have many questions."

Well, I sure did, and he started to answer them.

"Yes, Lou, you are correct. We could have destroyed the humans, but we did not. We are not a violent race and would not, then or now, use our technology to destroy life."

"And, Thomas, you are wondering why we did not return home. We had foreseen the rise of the machines. That is why many of us came to Earth centuries ago."

"Dr. Johnson, you are curious about the fate of both our people and yours. Those on the ship approaching Earth and those billions who inhabit the surface of Earth."

"Yes," said Johnson. "Time is short. We must communicate with the leaders of our world."

"That is not necessary. Even if it were, you would not succeed. Your people will not accept our people. They would only attempt to exploit our technology and, unfortunately, use it to either dominate or destroy other beings, human or alien. The time is not right for our people to meet."

"But," objected Johnson, "we..."

The voice ignored his objection. "We have planned for this day."

A wall on the other side of the room began to open. We stepped back.

A figure of average height and build stepped from behind it. He had a full head of hair and, indeed, looked like a human man in his mid-forties. He was dressed casually, in slacks, a shirt and a sportscoat. I was shocked. Thomas also appeared a bit taken aback.

"I am Ion." His lips were moving. "You have met three of our elders." He was referring to the short little guys. The Council has requested that I serve as your host. I will be assisted by Rey."

A beautiful young woman stepped forward."And Zeno."

A handsome young man appeared from behind Ion.

"Griff, a recent arrival from the surface will also assist them."

Griff appeared to be very much human. A white beard. Overweight. In his seventies, I would guess. Average height.

"As with all guests, you will receive a tour and an orientation toour world while we prepare for the arrival of the mothership, which we anticipate in two days. You will be asked to decide at that time if you wish to stay with us, as many of our guests have chosen to do or return to the surface.

"We have spent many years preparing for this day. We have created a world for our new arrivals."

A large yellow curtain was drawn back. Stretching out for what looked like miles was a city, or maybe just a large village. With trees and gardens and roads and even a couple of ponds or small lakes. What appeared to be the sky was light blue and cloudless. Some of the trees, which appeared to be evergreens, swayed in a lightbreeze. It was afternoon. Late afternoon. The light was fading. A bright yellow sphere appeared to be "setting" on the horizon. Peoplewere walking along the lanes. Children played in the yards andfields. We could hear no sound through the thick glass that separated us from the inhabitants of this world.

Our group was speechless, to say the least.

Now, I did know something about what these folks were talking about. I'm smarter than some people think. I'd read in the paper just before we left that the Japanese, who are very concerned about climate change and rising sea levels, had been funding a project bya corporation called Shimizu. They call it "Ocean Spiral." Apparently, they've been working on it for years and are planning to actually open it in the next few months. It's been built underwater in a deep part of the Sea of Japan, I think. They plan to house up to twenty thousand people.

Ion said that we would see their underwater world. Farming and mining. He told us that much of the facility's power came from methane produced by microorganisms on the ocean's bottom. And that they also took advantage of the ocean winds, meaning the currents, and temperature differentials at different levels to produce power.

And, of course, as Johnson pointed out, their technology was far ahead of ours. Japan's Ocean Spiral was only in the early stages of development. But these . . . people . . . yes, people, were already farming the ocean floor, and they weren't just planning to mine the ocean for minerals; they'd been doing it for hundreds of years.

"Yes, I know you have many questions, and we will answer themin time, but I am sure that you are weary from the day's endeavors and may want to rest," said Ion. "Rey and Zeno will show you toyour quarters." What was with this tour and orientation business? Where the hell were we? Disneyland? I was beginning to feel a little claustrophobic and was having some difficulty breathing. Maybe it was just anxiety. I inherited that from my mom. She always freaked out in closed spaces. Make a decision to "stay with us." I don't think so.

"Come," Zeno said, motioning to me and Jay. He turned and began walking while still talking. We followed him down a long hallway that led to what looked like an airlock. We stepped in, and the doorclosed with a loud bang. Zeno pushed the button marked LI.

"This is the level of the complex you could see from our viewing platform"

We stepped out into a twilight world. "It is almost five o'clock."

I checked my watch. He was right.

"Level I is set to Atlantic time. We raise and lower the light level tocorrespond to the time of day and the season." He smiled. "Members of our community who were surface dwellers live on this level. Soon it will be dark, and the fall constellations will appear. I believe that tonight we will have a new moon."

"How do you do that?" I asked. "Very simple. We use a large projection device, similar to your planetariums."

"Oh" I said. I'd only ever been in one planetarium when we visitedBoston with the girls.

"Let us get you to your rooms. They are adjoining." "Where are…"

"Your friends?" Zeno finished my question. "Do not worry, Thomas is receiving medical attention, and Rey has taken the doctors by one of our laboratories . . . aquatic, I believe. They willbe along shortly. They have rooms on the same floor. Every resident and guest of Home has their own room." Said Zeno.

"How long have you been here?" I asked. "I was born here thirty-five years ago."

"But you're not . . ." Jay began.

"Like the others? My father is Peruvian. My mother's parents were members of the first colony that we established on the ocean floor."

"How is that possible?" I asked.

"Genetic engineering. The council and our scientists decided a few centuries ago that those in love should be allowed to reproduce,even if they were of different species. Our bodies are not the same as either the human species or my mother's. Our physicians, however, have become quite skillful in treating the diversity ofpatients they serve." He stopped and motioned to two doors. "Settle in, and I will meet you in an hour for dinner."

The rooms were basic. A double bed, small bureau, a chair and desk with a lamp, a lounge chair, small closet, and a device that looked like a small computer.

Our bags were in our rooms. We opened the adjoining door and talked while we unpacked.

"Well, what do you have to say to this, Jay? I told you thatThomas was one the level."

She didn't respond, so I went to the door and asked again.

"I don't know," she said, and I'm sure she didn't. Neither did I.

When Zeno returned, I asked him about the small computers inour rooms.

"Yes, they are computers. We use them sparingly and do not text or email, unless the information cannot be communicated easily in person or in writing. We still instruct our children in handwriting, which I believe most of your schools no longer teach. We do not have a Facebook equivalent. We have a relatively small population and encourage in-person dialogue.

"How many residents?" I asked. "One thousand, two hundred, and six. With the new arrivals, we will be rethinking our use of communication devices."

"Twenty-two thousand is a lot more than one thousand, two hundred, and six."

"Yes, but we will still want to preserve   face-to-face communication. We do carry small communication devices to use when needed, usually to reach someone on another level.

"We will proceed to the dining hall. Most meals are communal, although each housing unit has a kitchen and dining room large enough for a family or group of friends." He waved his hand in the direction of a kitchen and dining room. "Griff will join us for dinner."

Jay and I asked more questions as we walked toward the dining hall, a large building in the center of the housing units. "How many levels do you have in this complex?"

"Nine at present, but only three are occupied.""Are they the same as this?" asked Jay.

"The living units are similar and have communal dining. The biggest difference is that the other levels have no day-night cycle; they remain dark all the time. I and those like me are engineered so that our eyes operate effectively on all seven levels."

"You mean that there's perpetual night on other levels?" "Yes. The residents and those who work there have no need for light. As I am sure you have noticed, those from my mother's planet have much larger eyes that have evolved in such a way as to detect heat patterns, not light."

We crossed the campus, as he called it, and moved through the door of the dining hall. Some children were playing what looked like soccer on the lawn outside. They looked normal. I mean, like Jay, me, and Zeno.

The dining room was noisy. A lot of people talking. Some inSpanish, maybe, but many in other languages that I also didn't understand.

"I bet they're serving fish," I said and chuckled."Yes," said Zeno. I don't think he caught it.

"Fish," I said again.

Jay just shook her head, but I could see a tiny smile.

"This is cafeteria style," said Zeno as he handed me a tray. I will help you with the selections tonight. We have fish every night, but we also have lamb and beef dishes, mainly for those from your world."

The fish didn't look like anything that I'd ever seen. Zeno said it was good, so I tried it. He was right. The beef tasted like beef. There were also a lot of vegetables that were unfamiliar. Some of them were pretty colorless. I did find something that looked and tasted like broccoli.

"Most of our vegetables come from the sea. We will go to the viewing platform for undersea farms tomorrow. We will also visit the farms on Level I, where the cattle and sheep are raised and the green vegetables you like are grown."

Griff joined us halfway through the meal. He sat down and immediately began to talk.

"Well, I'm sure you want to know how I got here. I was on my lobster boat, lost power, and was taking on water. Suddenly, the water around me started to boil, and my boat began to spin. I didn'tknow what was happening. Soon, I was surrounded by a wall of water. The boat descended, and I found myself here. They saved mylife, and the lives of many others: lost pilots, the crews of many ships, like the one from my hometown. I've met them. They're livinghere."

"The Carol Deering?" I asked."You know it?" asked Griff.

"Well, yes," I answered. "It was a 'ghost ship' that went aground off Cape Hatteras in the early years of the twentieth century, with no crew aboard. It was owned by a company that still operates in Portland."

"You're from Portland?"

"Yes, I grew up there. Have a house there."

"I worked there for years but never lived in the city. Couldn'tafford it."

I felt apologetic; I don't know why. "I bought before the market went completely crazy."

"Oh yeah, I remember. The late eighties and nineties. Too rich for my blood." He paused then went back to his story. "I thought about going back, but I didn't. After being here a while, I decided to stay."

"Why?" I asked.

"They're doing important things here. Not just plucking people out of the sea but trying to change our world. Trying to save it from itself. You must agree that we're in a downward spiral."

"Well, I don't know. I guess some would say that." I didn't knowwhat else to say. Jay didn't say anything.

"Oh, come on!" retorted Griff.

"Griff," said Zeno, "he does not have to agree with you." "Oh, yeah, the code. Sorry.""What code?" I asked.

"We ask all residents to abide by a code that requires us to respect others' opinions, even if they are quite different from our own. Acceptance of difference is one of the cornerstones of our society. Diversity of thought has allowed us to survive and makes our community resilient. Zeno seemed to want to say more, but, before he could, we were joined by a man in his early forties, balding slightly, with large, black-rimmed glasses.

"Hi Zeno, Griff," he said. "Are these some new arrivals?""Yes," answered Zeno.

"I'm Howard," he said. "I'm a retread."

"Howard means that he has returned to our colony. He came back after the accident at Pine Grove," Zeno explained.

Howard was there, like Brazil, I thought. It's a small world, or maybe I should say universe.

"So, do you folks think you'll stay?" asked Howard. "I wouldn't lie to you, I love Home. I'll never leave again. Shouldn't have yearsago, but I wanted to go back. Shouldn't have; I just ended up homeless and, on the streets, again." Zeno answered his question. "I must show them the rest of Home,and then they will decide if they will stay with us."

"Well, if you've got any questions, I'm always around." With that, Howard floated off to another table.

When he was out of earshot, I asked, "What's his story?"

"Howard came to us a few years ago. He was a deckhand on a cargo ship and fell overboard. Just by chance, one of our crafts was nearby and picked him up," said Zeno.

"And this last time?"

"That is more complicated. Howard initially chose to return to the surface. Shortly thereafter, one of our monitoring crafts crashed near Pine Grove. White Forks, actually," Zeno responded.

"What were you monitoring?"

"The development of your nuclear industry. We have been quite concerned since the use of nuclear weapons in your world war and the renewed interest of your government and billionaires in space exploration.

"We managed to rescue the two-member crew but not the craft. Howard found it, moved it, and somehow repaired it. He is quite brilliant. He managed to pilot it back by activating the homing navigation mechanism. We were quite worried that the craft would fall into the wrong hands, so we were very pleased when Howard arrived with it. We owe him a debt of gratitude.

"You likely need to rest from your day," Zeno offered. "You are also welcome to visit the art exhibit in the common area, and our small symphony is playing some original music."

I looked at Jay. "Well, we are tired, but I'd like to walk around some." Jay nodded.

"Certainly," replied Zeno. "Enjoy your walk. I will call for you at eight tomorrow. After breakfast, I will show you our farms andshops. We grow or make most of what we use here, but we do import a few items from above."

"How do you do that?" I asked.

"We have a very successful company on the surface. Our agents purchase certain goods that our transport crafts carry here."

Jay and I wandered through the art exhibit. I think Jay liked it. I've never cared much for modern art, and that's what I'd call this. I didn't understand it but smiled and nodded a lot.

We walked around the campus. The evening lights were coming on. The layout of our "sector," as Zeno called it, was relatively simple. Much like a Midwestern town. A to Z was East to West. One to twenty-five was North to South. Our living unit was B7. In the center of the complex was a park. It even had a duck pond with realducks! The air was warm and dry. There seemed to be a slight prevailing wind from the west.

The row of shops had already closed for the evening, so we lookedthrough the windows. There were a couple of women's shops, a men's store, a shoe store, a hardware, and a grocery. Some of the clothing items we didn't recognize, but many we did: dresses, pants, sweaters, suits, and sunglasses. Others were funny-looking, like a hat that looked like a cross between a top hat and a diving mask. And what looked like a black tuxedo made out of wetsuit material. I recalled Zeno telling us that some couples chose to get married on the ocean floor. Why not? We didn't see a wedding dress, but I assumed that they were custom-made and quite interesting.

People were sitting outside a couple of cafés. Live music was coming from one. And the people: they were a diverse mixture. Old and young. Some indigenous people from Peru, I assumed. Some English natives. Brown, yellow, and gray skin. Descendants of the original colony members. They all seemed to be enjoying themselves. There was a lot of conversation and laughter, but I didn't have a clue what they were saying. I couldn't understand a word of it.

More music wafted to us from a small open-air stadium just off thepark. Given that the weather didn't changed much on Level I, they had no need for an indoor venue. I guess it was like living in LA year-round, minus the wildfires, mudslides, and earthquakes. Atleast I assumed that there weren't any earthquakes.

We sat on a park bench on a hill overlooking the sunken stadium and enjoyed music that we'd never heard before from instruments we'd never seen. I can't really describe the sounds. I guess soft and peaceful, which is certainly what we needed. I don't really know much about music. My mother said that I couldn't carry a tune in a bucket. But I liked what I heard.

We didn't talk much. I guess we were just in shock. I mean, we were tired, but it was more than that: This world was real!

I slept pretty well that night. Jay stayed in her room, and I stayed in mine. She said that she needed some alone time, and I felt the same way.

CHAPTER 13

We were up and ready by eight. Jay and I had a quick breakfast in the dining hall. I don't think I could ever get used to eating fish for breakfast. Thank God, they had some scrambled eggs. At least I think they were chicken eggs. Maybe not.

Zeno was on time. This time he arrived in a . . . I guess it was a space-age golf cart. It looked sort of like some of those goofy golf carts that people in places like the Villages in Florida drive around. He said it would save us some time and was good for their environment.

We saw a bunch of sheep and cattle and llamas and alpacas. The place looked like your average American family farm. Zeno said that at only a couple hundred acres, it was much smaller than most modern corporate farms in America. When we got to the dairy farm, they were milking in one barn with what looked like modern, state- of-the-art equipment. The animals appeared healthy and larger thanthe ones I remember. But what do I know?

"Due to genetic engineering," Zeno said, "our farms are small butvery productive."

The farm fascinated me. "This is unbelievable!" I said.

"Yes," said Zeno, "that is what most new arrivals say. They oftenthink that our community, our world, is part of a dream."

"How…"

"Did we create a world like this under the sea? The basic technology from the colony is very old. It was developed by our ancestors on their ancestors' planet a few thousand years ago.Colonies like our own were developed on the bottom of Home'sGreat Sea.

We walked across the pasture to another barn.

"Of course, the technology for Level I was developed over the pastfive hundred years, so it is relatively new. We are still makingadvances, and production per acre continues to increase."

We entered the barn. A woman with brown skin and dark hair was shoveling cow shit out of a stall.

"This is Marie, one of our chief managers. She is charged with overseeing all food production for Level I. Marie, these are two new arrivals. Lou and Jay."

"Pardon me if I do not shake your hand," she said. "I can see that you have your hands full." I smiled.

She smiled back. "As I heard Zeno tell you, food production per acre is rising, but I fear not fast enough. Although our goal is self-sufficiency, we remain dependent on the surface people for much of our grain for the cattle, and we are quite concerned about the future. Your people may soon destroy their world."

"I see," said Jay. "This job looks hard. Long hours?"

"Yes, the work is strenuous at times, but I enjoy the challenge. All residents work on average four to six hours a day, and we are all paid the same wage."

"How will your work be affected by the large number of new arrivals who'll be entering your world in a few days?" I asked.

"I do not think that Level I will be affected that much. The new residents will be settled on levels four through seven. I believe that our planners have developed a system for integrating them into the larger society. Our people have anticipated their arrival for some time." "What kind of system?" I asked.

"We will interview and assess new arrivals in terms of their interests and skills," replied Zeno. "Based on that assessment, they will receive a work assignment for the next six months, while they are involved in some type of training program. We certainly want to train many of these arrivals in the sciences and mathematics, in which we assume they are quite deficient. As we do with ourchildren, we will use positive reinforcement to encourage their mastery of the education that we provide. It will be quite an impressive undertaking. As I said, we have been planning this for years. As I understand it, it will involve an orientation process that will focus on teaching the basic skills involved in self-control. We will talk more about these skills when you visit our school this afternoon.

"It sounds like a reeducation program," I said."Yes, you could say that" Zeno replied.

I didn't say anything more or ask further questions. It sounded likebrainwashing to me. More of having to "think the right way" stuff.

A young man approached us. "This is Gonzalo," Maria said.

"I regret to disturb you," he said, "but we are having some problems with the new equipment in the milking barn." "Well, I must go," apologized Maria. "Perhaps we can talk more later."

"Thank you," we said.

"Well, I'm very impressed with the farm," I said.

"Those who live on Levels II and III have a very different diet thanyours. They primarily eat what grows in the sea. So will the new arrivals, so we do not foresee having to expand this level.

With that, we proceeded to the viewing platform for the undersea farms, which I would have to say were equally impressive. Zeno switched on a couple of large spotlights that illuminated a small part of the operation. Neither the plants nor the farm workers required light. Much of the cultivation, which consisted of what appeared tobe pruning and weeding, was being done by robots directed by workers in heavy-looking pressure suits with large metal helmets similar to those in the movie **Twenty Thousand Leagues Under the Sea**. The large, leafless, colorless plants swayed with the current. Aswith those at dinner the night before, they didn't appear that appetizing to me. But Zeno said they were filled with all sorts of wonderful vitamins and nutrients. That afternoon, we visited the main school. Like at the café, the school had a mixture of descendants of the colony; indigenouspeoples of Peru and the Amazon, and folks like Zeno—the products of mixed marriages and genetic engineering. A liberal's wet dream.

"What do they study here?" Jay asked.

"Mathematics and science are obviously very important for our survival, but we also spend a great deal of time on the humanities: psychology, sociology history, and ethics. We focus on teaching our children self-control at a very early age, in preschool."

"Self-control—you teach that in preschool?" I asked.

Zeno looked puzzled. "Yes, of course. It is part of our core curriculum, whether for our preschoolers or new arrivals. The ability to control basic impulses is key."

"I thought you just learned that growing up. No one taught me." "Some do learn it by themselves, but many do not."

"Well . . ." I didn't know what to say to that. Perhaps if I'd learnedthat lesson better myself, I wouldn't be in the mess I was in with Lynn and my girls and Jay.

Zeno just looked at me for a moment and then went on with the tour. "We hope to instill a set of values and beliefs that will serve individuals well throughout their lives." "What values?"

"Fairness, gratitude, respect for difference and culture."

"Do you have sports teams? That's a great way to teach values."

"Not in the sense with which you are familiar. We do not encourage competition among peers, only within ourselves."

"Sounds to me like some pretty 'liberal' values," I whispered to Jay."We do not use punishment, because we learned long ago that it does not work. Our approach is similar to the teachings of your Jesus Christ."

Oh boy, I thought, we're getting into religion now. My Jesus Christ?

"Well, if punishment doesn't work, what does?" I felt my blood pressure rising.

"Positive reinforcement. We reward people for what they do. Psychologists have been writing about and applying this method for many years."

"Well, yes, I guess." I said. I wasn't going to argue the point. But Istill think a good rap up the side of the head can work wonders.

The last stop for the day was the medical center. It was a large building, but not much was happening there.

"Why isn't it busier?" asked Jay. "We teach people how to care for themselves. There is no drug abuse here. We are serious about preventive care and believe that healthcare is a right, not a privilege."

"Healthcare as a right? I don't know if I agree with that," I said. "I've always worked hard and gone without so that my family could have healthcare. I've always felt angry at those who got it fornothing. For no work and effort."

"We have many good reasons why we treat it as a right. Separate from ethical considerations, we need all our people to be healthy and productive. That benefits everyone. We all work here to support our community and to care for ourselves and each other.

"But doesn't it cost more to do it your way? Doesn't it mean an increase in taxes for everyone?"

"We do not pay taxes, Lou."

"No taxes? Well, I guess I'd be out of a job down here, given thatI spend most of my time doing people's taxes." I was getting a little irritated with all this liberal BS, so I snapped, "How the hell do you pay for things?"

"We pay for what we need mostly through our labor and the application of our knowledge and skills. We do use the revenue from our surface company to purchase what we cannot produce ourselves."

"And it works? I don't believe it."

"Join us, and we will make a believer of you."

"I know," I responded. "That's what I'm afraid of." Jay and I laughed, but Zeno looked confused again.

"So, you don't use money here?" I asked.

"No, just labor credits. Your accounting skills could be applied there. We have a system of keeping track of them, but any system can use improvement."

Dinner was at six. We went to the dining hall again. Griff was waiting, and, this time, I had questions. After we got our trays, I began to ask them.

"Who runs this place?"

Zeno spoke first. "There is a counsel with representatives from each sector elected by ranked-choice voting. All candidates present their views and positions in forums that our residents must attend if they are to vote."

"You mean you go listen to the person you like?" asked Jay. "You must hear out the position of the person you do not like, as well as the person you like," explained Zeno.

"Okay, so they run the place?" Now we were getting somewhere.

"No, they choose managers to run the farms, shops, food services, etc. Managers and planners must have expertise in the areas they manage or plan."

I chuckled. "Well, that's certainly different from our political appointment system."

"Sounds like a good idea," offered Jay, "but where do they get their expertise and training?"

"Many in the schools and apprenticeships we operate and some in the universities on the surface."

Griff joined the conversation. He'd just been listening. I guess trying to size up me and Jay. To my surprise, Howard was nowhere to be seen.

"So, what about personal freedom?" I asked, looking at Griff. "What do you mean?" he countered.

"Well, it seems like the place is run pretty tight. A lot of managers," I said. "Yes, that is true," Zeno responded. "It has to be. We must be productive and efficient to survive."

"I understand," I said, "but what about the code? That codebusiness. Tell me more about it."

"The code has many facets. If you decide to stay, we will give you an orientation and answer all the questions you have," Zeno promised.

"But what are some of the things in the code?"

"As I pointed out to Griff yesterday, everyone has a right to their opinion and to be treated respectfully."

"Okay."

"All genders, species, and races must receive equal and fair treatment. Violence for any purpose except self-defense is prohibited. Everyone must work and, through their work, supportthe larger community."

I still wasn't feeling very clear about all of this. "Tell me more about how it actually works, Zeno.""What do you want to know?"

"What happens when people get into a fight?""A physical altercation?" "Well that, too, but what happens when people have a bigdisagreement, like with a coworker?"

"The managers usually handle that. They mediate the conflict."

"What if it does turn physical? Someone punches someone else, say?"

"As I told you, we are not a violent race. I cannot remember that happening in my short life."

"But what if it does?"

"The Manager of Public Order would decide how to deal with it. Hemight appoint a mediator."

"Okay, but what if one of them decided to sue the other?"

"We do not sue people here. We have no lawyers. Or courts, for that matter. If you want an advocate for your position, the council will appoint one. You choose the advocate you would like; you only have to ask. The advocate will help you present your side of the argument."

"What happens if somebody steals something or kills a person?"

"Council members would decide what happens if the Manager of Public Order asked them to become involved. I cannot recall anyone being killed intentionally in my lifetime. Residents have been killed, but only in accidents." "This Manager of Public Order is like a police officer or constable?"

"They are similar, to some degree, although our Manager of Public Order has little to do. He works as a baker most of the time."

This, too, was starting to sound to me a lot like communism, and I didn't want any of that. Where was individualism and being able to keep the fruits of one's labor? What about your rights? A manager for this and a manager for that, and little or no crime. I had a hard time believing that one.

"People here want to support the code and the community, because it gives them freedom," said Griff.

"But all of these planners and managers?" I asked, shaking my head.

"It's not planning that infringes on freedom but planning that uses force. If you live here, you won't be forced to follow any plan, unless you want to. but you'll want to."

I didn't want to disagree with Griff or get into an argument. I guess I didn't really understand what he was saying. Maybe if I'd grown up on the bottom of the sea, I would've understood.

CHAPTER 14

Jay and I walked to the shops after dinner. She'd seen something in the window the night before that she wanted to try on. I'd heard someone at dinner say that the stores were open one night a week, and this was the night. She wanted me to go with her, so I did. But I wasn't interested in looking at women's clothing, so I told her I was going to walk over to the other side of the square. As I crossed the square, I heard footsteps behind me.

"Wait up!" a voice said. I turned. It was Howard.

"Well, I heard from Zeno that you saved the day a while ago," Isaid.

"Oh, you mean about bringing their craft back to Home? Well, Iwouldn't lie to you, I guess I did. It was pretty easy."

"For you," I said. "I wouldn't have a clue." Never could even fix abicycle, much less a spacecraft.

"Well, stay, Lou. It is Lou, isn't it?" I nodded.

"I'll teach you," he said.

"It's a little hard to teach old dogs new tricks."

"No, I don't think so. I had to learn new things when I came back. I had to get rid of all that anger I'd been carrying around for years. They helped me with that. And I had to learn to trust other people. Never had. Had no real good reason to, but now I do. I'm telling you,Lou, it's not as hard as you think."

"I don't know. I've got reasons to go back. I have a mess back there that I need to clean up."

"Well, you have to do what you think is right. I did, and Home is right for me."

"I'll think about it, Howard. I appreciate your offer."

"I mean it. You know I mean it. Just look me up if you stay. E-7, okay?"

"Okay," I said, and Howard was gone.

When I got back to the shop, Jay had something to show me. She hadn't bought anything; the woman wouldn't accept her money. But she'd given Jay an alpaca scarf. It was the softest thing I'd ever touched. We walked down to the pond. We hadn't talked much, and I thought we should.

"What do you think, Jay?" I asked. "We could certainly disappear here like apparently others have done. Zeno said that we have a meeting with Ion and the boys tomorrow morning."

"I know," said Jay. "Well?" I said.

"I don't know."

She was avoiding answering me. "Jay . . . "

"Look, I can't make this decision for you. You're the one who wanted to leave it all behind. I was pretty happy putting up stock in Jane's toy store. I didn't need this."

I didn't like a lot of it. Seemed like groupthink. Communism. I'd haveto change a lot to live here, which I could have done, but . . . it seemed just too much for me. Plus, I'd likely never see my kids or Lynn again.

I really needed to talk to Jay like we used to talk, but she felt closed to me. Just like other times when she would shut me out, because she was angry with me. But why would she be angry with me now? I didn't know what was going on. She'd said very littlesince we'd arrived. And that wasn't like her. She usually had an opinion that eventually came out. I started to feel like she'd given up on me, maybe a long time ago, and I'd just refused to recognize it.

"Do you like it here?" I asked.

"It's okay," she said. She sounded angry, but I wondered if shewas more scared than anything.

"Do you want to stay?"

Her one-word answer was immediate: "No."

"Okay," I said, "can you tell me why? I know that neither of usever dreamed of living in such a world."

"No." she said.

I waited.

"It just doesn't feel like home to me."

What could I say to that? We sat for a long time in silence.

"Well, I'm ready to go," said Jay. I didn't object. We walked back without a word except "goodnight" when we reached our doors. I went to bed but couldn't sleep. I kept thinking about Lynn and the kids and Jay. I just couldn't see me abandoning all of it, or Jay and me spending the rest of our lives in this little underwater utopia. Throughout the night, I kept muttering to myself, "Too much. Too much." Finally, morning came.

Breakfast was rushed, and, even though we were running late, I stillhad to wait for Jay. You know how women can be. Men are always waiting on them. I yelled through the door that I was going down to what they called the communal kitchen. I noticed coffee in there yesterday.

When I got there, I poured myself a cup of coffee, added two creams, and sat down to wait. To my surprise, Griff was at the next table

"Can I join you?" he asked.

"Sure," I said, "pull up a chair."

Once he changed seats, I posed a question. "May I ask why you didn't go back?"

"You may." He chuckled. "I didn't have enough reasons to go back.No job. No real family. Oh, I had some good friends up there, but noreal reason to stay. Here I have a purpose. I'd lost that up there.

Plus, I like these people, and they like me. They've got energy and direction, and I need that. I'm telling you, think about it."

I heard Jay. "Come on, Lou. Zeno's here. We need to go." "Coming," I yelled then turned back to Griff.

"Well, you heard the boss." He smiled."I'll think about what you said."

"Sure," he said.

"Hey, I waited on you," I said to Jay before starting down the hall.

"It wouldn't kill you to wait on me for a minute."

I wished that I could've talked to Griff more. I don't know, maybe I'd have made a different decision. He seemed to understand some things that I didn't. He was a bright fellow. Much brighter than me. He seemed to have thought through all of this. But he didn't have a reason to go back. No wife. No kids. I did. I just don't know. God, I do say that a lot.

Zeno said that our meeting with Ion had been moved up and that we'd have to declare our intentions about staying a bit earlier than we'd planned. So, we should pack, I thought. He picked us up at 9:30 and delivered us to the elevator to Level II. We thanked him for his hospitality and asked him to give our regards to Griff, Howard, and the others.

I pushed the button for Level II. The boys, Thomas included, were waiting for us. Thomas looked much better. The rest and medical attention had done him good. We hadn't seen much of them since we'd arrived. Just in passing. They were all talking with Rey, who moved us down the hall to a meeting room. Ion was there already.

"I hope that you have enjoyed your brief visit with us and have gained an understanding of who we are. As you may have heard from your guides, we created many of your mysteries—the Nazca Lines in Peru, the stone statues on Easter Island—yet your people reject even the idea that we exist. And you will have no proof to the contrary, so they will not believe you if you choose to go back and relate what you have seen here."

"Unfortunately, we have increasing concerns regarding your people, such as your continuing advances in technology. We hope that you do not make the mistake we made of letting technologyturn you into a disconnected leisure class that will eventually be controlled by the technology you created. Your continued fascinationwith nuclear war and space exploration are also major concerns, as is your tendency to choose narcissists and sociopaths to run your governments. If you continue down this path, you will weaken and destroy democratic governments' ability to govern. Your world will be controlled totally by dangerously large corporations and billionaires."

"We have been discussing that your world—indeed, the universe—needs our people to become active again in changing the directionof history. Not through violent means, but by encouraging tolerance for difference and increasing your ability to appreciate aspects of existence other than individual achievement and the personal acquisition of wealth. Our world is on the right side of history: the history of the universe.

"Now, for the other reason that I asked you to meet me this morning. We must communicate with your ship, Thomas. The approach to Earth must come out of the sun so that the surface people will be aware of the craft only for a short time before it appears to crash into the sea."

"Yes," replied Thomas. "My crew and I agreed to that trajectory before we left the mothership."

Ion continued. "The ship must appear to be destroyed; neither the humans nor the machines can have any knowledge of our world. Unfortunately, our transmitters here are not strong enough to contact your ship, and those on the small crafts that leave here only work within the Earth's atmosphere. Dr. Johnson, might you andDr. Carson be able to help us with this?"

"Yes, yes. I believe we can," Johnson replied.

As usual, Jay and I didn't know what the old man and his colleagues were up to. Johnson, Carson, and Raymond immediately went into a huddle in the corner. They were whispering—why, I have no idea, since these guys could read thoughts. We were the only two who didn't know what was going on. So, we strolled over and listened.

It seemed that they'd once worked at a NASA research facilitynear Cape Canaveral that had seen little use since their departure. They thought that they could manage to get in and use the radio- transmitter equipment. Security "was pretty lax" at night and on weekends. They would contact Thomas's clan, arrange for the "crash," and everyone would live happily ever after on the bottom ofthe sea. Except maybe me and Jay.

Johnson, Carson, and Raymond seemed fine with returning to the colony. I'm sure that they could keep busy with their science experiments for the rest of their days. If they came back, no one would believe them anyway. They'd already been discredited. And they had no proof.

So, we could come along for the ride, and, after everything was over, they'd drop us off in Cocoa Beach. The colony folks, they said, wouldn't release us until Thomas's clan had been brought safely aboard—or whatever you call it.

"So, what about us being exposed to something?" I asked Johnson.

"Oh, don't worry about that. The scan they gave you coming inand the one they'll give us going out will take care of that."

"What about Thomas?" He'd also been worried about disease.Prior to the crash, he'd not felt well and thought that he might be coming down with something terrible.

"Their medical team has given him the once-over and isn't concerned," said Johnson. "He'll also recover from his burns."

So, we could go home after the splashdown. Tell anyone anything we wanted. No one would believe us, either. After all, we weren't rocket scientists, if that would make any difference. People would think that we were just two more head cases from the Bermuda Triangle. For a moment, I thought about how life might be if we stayed with the colony folks. No one would ever know what had happened to us. We would just disappear. No questions to answer. But we'd never see our families again. At least by going back, I hada chance to see mine and maybe straighten things out. I really wanted to go back. Jay felt the same way. Maybe she did miss her sister.

Given that time was short, the visit to the old research facility would have to happen that night. So, arrangements were made. The mothership knew to approach from the sun, but the time and coordinates of splashdown would have to be sent to them.

The portal we used for the ride back to Cocoa Beach wasn't as large as the gateway we'd arrived through. But the ship that we were taking was straight out of The Day the Earth Stood Still. A for-real flying saucer, I swear.

Johnson decided to have the guys drop us in a somewhat isolated spot near an old strip club he used to frequent. He said that people there were always seeing strange things in the sky. No one ever paid any attention to them, though; they were usually half drunk when they made their reports. We could get a cab back to his house, pick up our car, and go from there. The ship's crew treated us well. They showed us aboard, gave us seats, and told us that we might experience some minor changes in pressure as we rose to the surface.

"Your ears may ring," one warned us. "Swallow frequently as we rise to the surface."

Lights flashed, the humming sound got louder, and soon the dark blue of the sea became the dark blue of the night sky. We could walk around the ship, so we peered out the windows. The sky was beautiful. The stars seemed brighter than I remembered them. There was no moon.

It wasn't long before we saw the lights of the coast. We appeared to be flying only a few hundred feet above the ocean. Johnson said that this was how they avoided radar detection.

The trip to Cocoa Beach had taken less than an hour. The craft slowly descended onto the beach. A door opened and a walkway lowered. Soon, we were standing in the sand. We could hear music coming from the club a few hundred yards away.

Without making a sound, the craft retracted the walkway and slowly began to rise and move off to the south. Our little party was on its own. Johnson said that we must hurry. We had little time to "do great things." Maybe they were. But from what Jay and I had seen, we were, yet again, just along for the ride.

We all walked in the direction of the music. Johnson; Carson; Raymond; Jay; I; and, yes, Thomas, who'd insisted on coming along.I was wondering how we were going to fit everyone into a cab. But Johnson said that wouldn't be a problem. A cab or two were minivans that brought a van full of guys from the retirement communities just over the hill.

We got back to Johnson's and picked up his SUV. Jay and I followedin my car. This would have been our time to escape, but we decided tosee things through to their end. It was getting late, which is what Johnson wanted. We followed the SUV into a side road. Johnson saidthat we should walk from there. But it seemed that the MIT boys weren't too sure how they were going to get past the old analog security system that was monitored at night by two guards at the main entrance.

This is where Jay and I stepped in and saved the day. I wondered if Thomas and the others knew that was going to happen and waswhy they insisted that we stay until the mothership landed. Maybe they could foretell the future as well as read minds. Jay knew how tocreate a diversion for the guards, and I knew something about analog alarm systems. I'd had a part-time job repairing them when Lynn and I needed extra money for the girls' education.

Jay took the SUV around to the front gate and stopped right in front of the guard station. She quickly rubbed a spot of lipstick on her arm, got out, popped the hood, and immediately began to work on the engine. I guess her uncle had been a mechanic and she was pretty comfortable around cars. The two guards, of course, became concerned. Jay left on the cell phone that Bert had given her so that I could listen in. One guard came over to find out what she was doing.

"Lady, you'll have to move your truck."

"Oh, I'm so sorry, Captain. I don't know what's wrong with it tonight. Overheated, I think, and I just burned my stupid arm on the manifold. She showed him the red spot. I hate to ask, but you don't happen to have an ice pack, do you? I don't want a nasty scar there. . . Oh, God, it really does sting."

"Jeff, can you bring out the first-aid kit?""Will do." "Why don't we let it cool off for a minute, and then you can try itagain. Jeff's coming with the ice pack."

"Oh, thank you, Captain. I'm so glad that you boys were here andwilling to help."

"Here you go. Put this on your arm."

"Oh, that feels so much better. Thank you, Jeff; you're a darling."

While she was chatting up the two guards, I bypassed the analog alarm system on the back gate, and we were inside.

It didn't take the guys long to accomplish their mission. They took control of the telemetry system and sent a message to the approaching ship. Bert then buzzed Jay on the cell phone, signaling that were finished and had gotten through the gate and onto the road behind the facility.

"Let me try it one more time." Jay got into the SUV and switched on the engine. It started.

"Thank you, boys." She handed the ice pack to first guard who'd come to her assistance. "You were lifesavers tonight. I'm sorry for causing you any trouble."

"No trouble, ma'am. Have a good night."

Jay drove off in the direction of the cargo gate. She pulled up, and we jumped in and headed for the beach. "What a performance!" I said, as we drove away.

So, I guess you could say that those acting gigs that Jay had done in community theater, and me having had that part-time job with the alarm company had paid off for all of us. Jay and I had finally managed to do something important. Something that mattered.

"It won't be long now," said Johnson.

I looked a little confused.

"Until the mothership crashes into the sea."

"You'll be able to see that from here?" asked Jay, voicing my thoughts.

"If you know where to look. The show won't be as good as it will be from the Carolinas or Bermuda. It'll look to them like a blazing fireball, a meteor. But we should be able to see it from here. We just need to look to the northeast."

It was close to five A.M. when we got back to where the craft had dropped us. We waited, staring out over the ocean. The water was calm, the night warm. It would be getting light in an hour or so.

"It should be entering the Earth's atmosphere about now," said Johnson. "Look! There it is!"

Silently, a small streak of light rapidly grew in brightness and intensity. Then it disappeared into the sea.

"That was it?" I asked.

"What'd you expect?" Johnson countered. "The overture from StarWars?"

"Well, I didn't know what to expect," I said.

The craft from the colony reappeared. They sent a visual signal to Thomas that the ship's arrival had gone well, and that Jay and I could leave if we were not returning with them.

Good-byes aren't easy for anyone, I guess. I've never been very good at them, anyway.

"Well," said Johnson, seeming to be at an uncharacteristic loss for words, "I appreciate what you kids have done. I'm not sure we could've done it without you." He chuckled, sounding a bit apologetic. "Even though no one else will ever know about it." We nodded and smiled, and I shook hands with him, Raymond, and Bert.

"Are you sure that you guys will be okay, going back with Thomas?" "We have no good reason not to. None of us has family or any other ties, really," said Bert.

Raymond nodded. "And it's a chance of a lifetime for all of us." Jay gave hugs all around.

The hardest one to leave was Thomas, our little carjacker, or should I say starjacker, as Jay called him. There's a word for what we were feeling. It has to do with developing affection for one's captor and tormentor. Jay said it was called Stockholm Syndrome. She read about it in one of her women's magazines. But Thomas hadn't tormented us. Of everyone,he seemed to best understand the demons we were wrestling.

"Well, my friend, I don't know if I'll see you again. I wish you and your clan all the best."

Jay nodded. I could see that she was beginning to cry. I was surprised. She hugged Thomas. I did, too, even though I'm not a hugger.

Thomas made eye contact with me with those big black eyes. He smiled. "My people and I are very appreciative and grateful for the kindness that you have shown us. We will forever be in your and Jay's debt." We didn't really know what to say to that, so we didn't sayanything; we just smiled.

"I know that you and Jay will be returning to your homes. My people and I certainly understand the importance of home. You must create it wherever you are. I hope that you will do that when you return to your work and families." Still looking me in the eyes, he said, "Do the right thing."

With that, Thomas followed Johnson, Bert, and Raymond up the ramp and into the ship. It was starting to get light when the craft pulled away. Jay and I watched until it was out of sight.

CHAPTER 15

Well, I've been sitting here in this bar in the Melbourne, Florida airport all afternoon, talking to a lot of different people, but mostly to you. My flight back home has been delayed again. That's why I'vehad all this time to tell you my story.

I let Jay have the car for the week. We hadn't talked much since we'd seen the boys off. She said that she really needed a vacation after all we'd gone through. She rented a condo on the beach and will drive back home in a week. I booked the earliest flight to Maine that I could find.

We talked a little it the car this morning before she dropped meoff.

"Lou, you know, you could stay with me for the week. Maybe you need some time to get your head together before you go back?"

"No, no, I think I've been away long enough. I want to go home and face the music. Better now, I think, than later." "Okay," she said, and that was that.

We pulled up at the drop-off, and I got out. She got out. He hugged each other, but not really. I stood there, feeling like I should say something, but, as usual, I didn't. Jay didn't, either. She just got back in the car and drove off. I guess we'll see what happens when we finally get home.

Well, at least Jay and I finally got to do something that mattered, even if only our small group of humans and aliens would ever know about it.

We both picked up new cellphones. Thomas had lost ours in the mad dash we made to leave Peru and our friendly neighborhood drug dealer Ricardo far behind. Jay called her friends to let them know that she was okay. I haven't called anyone yet. What I need tosay I'm sure I need to say in person.

It's been a week or so since I've seen Lynn. I've lost track of time.The sad thing is that I don't really miss her. Well, I mean I don't reallymiss talking to her. I miss my conversations with my dog Walter andmy friend Joe more. I guess that's been the problem for years. I don'tfeel the things that I think I should feel toward Lynn. Now, that's nottrue with everyone. I miss my kids and . . . I hesitate to say it, but I miss Jay. Now, what do I do about that? I don't know. I don't have to go back. God knows Lynn may say, "Good riddance." And I'd understand if she did. In fact, I might feel relieved. I mean, I love the woman and care about her, but . . . well,I guess the "but" is the problem. It has been for a long time.

I just don't have a place in Lynn's life anymore. She's got her career and her women friends. And me, I've got Walter. I'm not trying to sound sorry for myself, but that's how I really feel.

Even what's happened hasn't resolved that for me. But it hasmade things a lot clearer. I'm very tired. Burned out. God knows, I need a change. Maybe I can make that change with Lynn if I commit myself to it and to her. And if I can't—if we can't—then maybe we need to end the marriage. But not this way. Jay was right. Lynn and my kids deserve better than this.

And work. I don't know about work. The same old job? I don't think so. They probably wouldn't have me back anyway. I need something different. Something that's worth doing and provideshealth insurance, given the mess that the boys and girls in Washington have made of it. I guess change for change's sake aloneisn't always good. I keep thinking that maybe I should do somethingthat involves helping people. Now, I know that sounds warm and fuzzy, and that's not me. At least, it's never been me. I don't know. Maybe I've changed in some ways. Stranger things have happened.

As for the machines on the edge of our solar system, I hope they stay where they are. I think we all can agree that we humans have our hands full trying to control the machines that we've created. Hopefully, we'll do a better job of it than Thomas' clan.

Well, they're finally calling my flight. You've been a good listener.I gestured to the bartender. "What's the damage?"

He showed me the check, and I paid it."What's his name?" I asked.

"Jake," replied the bartender."He's yours?"

"Yeah, I've had him for seven years."

"He reminds me a lot of my retriever, Walter." I turned and gave Jake a final pat on the head.

Thomas' last words to me, "Do the right thing," kept echoing in my mind. Just like when he'd first gotten into my head. But this time it's different. I have a choice. I'd like to do the right thing. At least that's what I hope to do

.

ABOUT THE AUTHOR

Dr. Breazeale is a clinical psychologist who has worked in the field for over 30 years. He has developed and administered numerous mental health and substance-abuse programs and has written extensively in the field of psychology.

Breazeale writes about the things that he knows. He was bornwith a birth defect, the absence of a left hand, in the "Atomic City", Oak Ridge Tennessee, where his parents lived and worked. He has worn a prosthetic hook most of his life. Having grown up in theSouth as a child with a disability, Dr. Breazeale has focused much of his clinical practice and writing on those with a disability and their families. He worked briefly for the United States Government He andhis wife adopted their daughter in Peru when she was three months old in the middle of a major offensive against the government by the Shining Path, a communist-supported terrorist group. Most of Dr. Breazeale's wife's family died in the Holocaust.

Dr. Breazeale has developed a number of training programs, most recently "Duct Tape Isn't Enough" focused on the attitudes and skills of resilience.

He is married and has one child. He lives and works in southern Maine.